The Librarian

A Pirate's Revenge

Eric Hobbs

Kokomo, IN / Eric Hobbs – First Edition

ISBN 978-1718681781

Printed in the United States of America

For everyone who waited,
and those who were good enough to push.

PROLOGUE

THE LIBRARIAN WAS reading by candlelight the first time he felt his library shift from one reality to the next. He didn't know that's what had happened, of course. In fact, at the time he didn't know it could happen at all.

It began simply enough. Dust rained down from the rafters. His teacup rattled in its saucer, dancing across his desk as the building began to shake.

The Librarian leapt from his rocking chair. His joints weren't as stubborn as they would become, but he stumbled when the floor wavered beneath his feet nonetheless. He moved into the arched doorway, listening to the moan of protesting stone as the building rocked back-and-forth. For a moment, he thought the library might come down around him, but the quake ended as quickly as it began – lasting just long enough to send his tea over the edge to the floor.

Drat, he thought. *I was enjoying that.*

The Librarian stepped out of his study. He was ready to grab a broom for the broken china and a rag for the tea when he was sidetracked by something in the corridor just outside the door. A large painting had come unlatched from the wall to reveal one of the library's secret passageways.

The old man pushed the painting shut and secured the latch before starting into the building's main hall. If there was damage downstairs, he wanted to take care of it before the daytime employees arrived with their own thoughts about who could be called to fix things. He didn't want contractors poking around his library. He didn't want *anyone* poking around his library. This was how he liked it. He preferred to be alone, nothing but his books and his age-old duty to keep him company.

Although a few of the displays had been jostled, his survey confirmed the earthquake hadn't disturbed much downstairs. A sword had fallen from its place on the wall near the *Treasure Island* exhibit. An Indian headdress was laying on the floor beside the table of *Peter Pan* relics. Nothing major, nothing the ladies couldn't attend to when they arrived for work in the morning.

All at once, The Librarian sensed movement in the darkness behind him. He wheeled around. His gazed moved back-and-forth across the room. It hadn't been much. Something brushing past a stack of books, perhaps.

"Who's there? Come out where I can see you!"

Beams of pale moonlight streamed through a nearby window, but most of the building was ensconced in darkness. His imagination ran wild. He was like a kid in so many ways. That's why they'd chosen him, after all. His limitless imagination. His unbound creativity. Unfortunately, those things were working against him now...

What if the quake had opened one of the portals? Was that possible? If so, who knew what monstrosities might be lurking in the darkness. Maybe Grendel had fallen through the portal between worlds. Perhaps Medusa was slithering down one of the aisles with her headful of snakes ready to turn The Librarian to stone. It could be anything. Perhaps it was the monster that had kept him awake as a child: the Jabberwock from Wonderland.

"I know you're there!" he said. "Don't make me—"

This time The Librarian saw shadows move. He turned just in time to see a young boy dart toward the lobby.

"Stop! I see you! Stop there!"

The Librarian hurried after him. He prayed the boy was just some random kid who'd broken into the library on a dare. It happened. He'd often seen kids spying from across the street, older kids daring their friends to sneak inside and procure evidence to confirm the dark stories told about Astoria's librarian were true.

The old man rushed through the lobby and into the night but stopped short when he saw the boy was already in the street. He would never catch him. Besides, he'd seen enough. He'd only wanted to verify who'd broken into his library, and he'd been able to do that.

It hadn't been a monster from another world.

And it hadn't been some random kid off the street.

The sadness of a frown touched The Librarian's face. "Oh, Douglas," he said. "What have you done now?"

❖ ❖ ❖

Twelve-year-old Douglas Stanford looked back to find the library was already out of sight. He flashed a crooked grin and slowed from his all-out sprint to a quick walk. He'd gotten away with it. Sure, he'd hear an earful when he saw The Librarian again, but the old guy was always lecturing him about something.

He might as well have a little fun.

Truthfully, Douglas didn't understand what the big deal was. Did The Elders really expect him to spend his summer in the library without enjoying the magic they were training him to protect? Seriously? That wasn't going to happen.

Douglas zipped his jacket and turned the corner into his neighborhood. He cut through yards to make it home a bit quicker but slowed up when his house came into view.

Something wasn't right.

His dad's car wasn't in the driveway.

Douglas hurried across the street and jumped the fence. His parents had gone to bed an hour before he left. He didn't understand why they would have gotten up to leave. Unless...

Unless his sister had ratted him out.

Dang it, Kate.

Worry turned to anger as Douglas climbed the trellis to his bedroom window on the second floor. He'd been careful to leave the window open when he left for the library but saw it was now closed.

Probably locked me out, too. Brat!

Surprisingly, the window opened with little effort. Douglas climbed through then gently closed it behind him.

Convinced he was in the clear, Douglas kicked off his shoes and let his jacket fall to the floor. He was about to slink into bed when he saw something that stopped him dead in his tracks.

A pale arm was dangling over the side of his bed from beneath one of the blankets. Someone was sleeping in his bed!

"Hey!" His voice was just loud enough to rouse the girl from beneath his covers. She sat up, barely awake. "Kate! Get out of my room!"

Kate talked through a yawn with her eyes closed. "What do you want?"

"I want you to get your greasy head off my pillow!"

Kate stopped mid-stretch as if all her muscles seized up at the sound of her brother's voice. She wiped the sleep from her eyes and looked about. Then—

She shrieked. *"Oh my God! What are you doing?!"*

"Stop screaming! What's wrong with you?"

Kate stood up on her bed like she'd woken to discover a monster had stepped into the room from her closet. *"Mom! Dad!"*

"Oh! You're gonna tell? Really? Good! 'Cause I..."

His words trailed off. He hadn't noticed before, but his room was neater than he'd left it. Someone had re-arranged the furniture, too. His bed was in the right place, but everything else was different: the books on shelves, the toys placed neatly in bins, the knickknacks on his desk – none of it belonged to him.

Everything seemed *off*.

Just as this realization rooted itself in the boy's mind, Mr. Stanford barged into the room and hit the lights. His eyes landed on Douglas and registered shock just as Kate's had a few moments before.

"What are you doing in this house?" he exclaimed.

Douglas furrowed his brow. "Are you serious?"

Mrs. Stanford started into the room right behind her husband but stopped in the doorway when she saw Douglas. She instinctively covered her mouth with an open hand to keep from screaming in surprise.

Mr. Stanford grabbed Douglas by the arm as his wife hurried to help Kate down from her bed. *"Answer me! How did you get in my daughter's room!"*

"Dad!" Douglas whined. "Stop! This isn't funny!"

Tears welled in the boy's eyes. He tried to pull away, but his father refused to loosen his iron grip.

Finally, Mrs. Stanford spoke up. "Jackson, stop it.

He's scared to death."

"I don't care! He—"

"Take Kate downstairs."

"But—"

"Now, Jackson."

Mr. Stanford glared at Douglas then reluctantly let him go before turning to lead Kate out of the room.

Once they were gone Mrs. Stanford took a seat on the bed. She offered her hand to Douglas. "It's alright," she insisted. "C'mon."

While still upset, Douglas couldn't resist his mother. He needed her to help him understand what was happening. If this was all part of some radical punishment, he'd complain about that later. Right now he just wanted his mother's comfort. He took her hand and sat down on the bed beside her.

"What's his problem?" Douglas sneered.

"He's confused." His mother's tone soothed him like a warm glass of milk.

"*He's* confused?" Douglas asked. "Where's all my stuff?"

Without responding, Mrs. Stanford put an arm around Douglas so he could rest his head on her shoulder.

"I'm sorry I snuck out. I know I shouldn't have, but you guys didn't have to do all this. I mean... this is crazy."

"Where did you go, sweetheart?"

Douglas looked up at his mother. He wanted to tell her the truth. They were acting like he was some ordinary kid sneaking out to hang with friends. But he wasn't. Not anymore. They needed to know that...

Mom, Sleepy Hollow is a real place. I've been there. So is Neverland and Wonderland and Oz. They're all real. There's magic in the world, mom. It's my job to protect it. At least, it will be...

He'd tell her all that soon enough. He'd tell her, and for once, she'd be proud of him. For once, his parents would look at him the way they looked at Kate.

Douglas hung his head. "I was just walking around."

"Did something happen?"

"What do you mean?"

"Did you get hurt? Did you bump your head?"

Douglas sniffed his nose and wiped his tears. "No?"

"Can I ask you something? You have to promise you won't get upset. Whatever you say, we'll help you through this. You need to trust me so we can figure this out."

Douglas didn't like where this was going.

"Why did you sneak into this house? Are you hiding from someone? I give you my word we'll do what we can to help, but you have to tell us exactly what's going on."

Douglas jumped from the bed and backed away from his mother. "Stop! I get it, okay? I shouldn't have snuck out, but–"

"Sweetheart, if this is some sort of prank..."

"*I'm* pulling a prank? Okay, you're not my mom? This isn't my house? How come I know everything about you?"

"Such as?"

"Well... umm... grandma died last Christmas... how about that?"

Mrs. Stanford flinched.

"And... you play piano... and... and you coach Kate's soccer team. You try, at least. Oh yeah! The toilet down the hall never fills up when you flush it. Dad's been trying to fix it for years and won't let you call a plumber."

Mrs. Stanford stared at the boy in disbelief. She stood from the bed and started toward the door. "Wait here."

When she disappeared into the hall Douglas threw his arms up in disgust. Looking about, he couldn't believe they'd gone through so much trouble to change his room. The room was perfectly staged to look like Kate had been living there for years. None of his things had been left behind. They'd even–

They'd even painted the walls to match Kate's bedding.

Only that wasn't possible. They couldn't have painted the room that quickly. Even if they had, the room would smell of paint. Instead, it smelled like Kate's cheap, drugstore perfumes.

Douglas heard muffled voices from downstairs and started down the hall after his mom. He could tell his father was angry. He knew that tone of voice all too well. And his sister... she was crying. Why was she still acting scared?

Douglas tiptoed down the staircase and peered around the corner into the kitchen. His father was seated at the table with both arms draped around Kate. She had her face buried in his chest. She wasn't crying after all...

She was sobbing.

"I don't think he meant to scare you. He's just a little mixed up. Mom will take care of this."

Across the room, Mrs. Stanford was on her phone.

"Yes," she began, "I'm not sure who to call. We have... well... intruder isn't the right word... a young boy has broken into our house... but... he's confused."

Douglas dug his wallet out and stormed into the kitchen. When his parents saw him, both immediately stepped between Douglas and their crying child.

"You think you're so funny, don't you? You know what? The joke's on you. You've *always* treated Katie better than you treat me. All you did tonight was re-arrange my room." He opened his wallet and pulled an I.D. from inside. "A day will come when I'm *not* your kid, but right now I am. Here's the proof."

Douglas smirked. He knew his student I.D. would put an end to this little game once and for all. It had all his stats in case of emergency: his name, his picture, his address – everything – even parent-contact information. He looked down at the card before handing it over then pulled it back for a better look.

His stomach sank.

The card was blank. None of the information he expected was there. All that remained was an awkward school photo. But as he studied the card, even that began to fade, until there was nothing on the card at all.

Douglas let the blank I.D. drop from his trembling hand. Tears pooled in his eyes again. It was like his entire life was being erased...

As if he'd been written out of existence.

Douglas looked up sharply as something occurred to him. He replayed the night in his mind. He'd followed the rules – the important ones, anyway – but the library's magic was the only thing that could explain something like this.

The boy backed away from his family. His mother started after him.

"Wait," she said. "Don't go. It isn't..."

Douglas bolted out of the house before she could finish. He ran down the street, tears stinging his face the entire way. He was in trouble. Not the trouble you get into for sneaking out of the house. This was serious, the kind of trouble people can find themselves facing when they play with magic they don't fully understand... and refuse to follow all the rules.

CHAPTER 1

A GUST OF cold wind blew through the tent and woke Randy Stanford from a deep sleep. He was surprised the light breeze had been enough to wake him. After everything he'd been through, he felt like he could sleep for days.

Randy rolled onto his side and saw his dad was lying on a blanket beside him. His eyes were open and fixed on the overhead tarp. He seemed to be staring through it, as if his thoughts were on something so far away it existed beyond the night sky.

"Aren't you going to sleep?" Randy asked.

"Eventually," Douglas explained.

Randy crawled through the tent's open door and came to his feet.

They'd set up camp near the base of an old windmill that had seen better days. Two additional tents were pitched across from Randy. The rasping sound of someone's blubbering snore echoed through the early morning.

While the others were still asleep, Taylor had perched on a fallen log near the remains of the campfire that had kept them warm through the night. Randy walked over and took a seat beside her, but Taylor didn't look up to acknowledge his presence. She just kept her eyes fixed on the fire, her thoughts no doubt somewhere in the distance just like Randy's dad.

Randy sat in the uncomfortable silence for as long as he could before finally speaking up. "Why didn't you run?"

"Where am I supposed to go – find the Mad Hatter to have tea?"

The fire snapped and popped for a bit before he tried again.

"You ever go camping?"

Tay looked at him sideways, flabbergasted by the casual nature of his question.

"My dad, he loves to get out in the wilderness, says it reminds him of all the make-believe adventures he had as a kid. He takes me with him sometimes, but it's so boring I usually spend the whole time trying to get a signal on my phone."

"What are you doing?" Taylor asked.

"What do you mean?"

"Are we friends?"

Taylor held her icy gaze on Randy until he looked away.

"He's not as bad as you think," Randy muttered.

Taylor offered a snort of mock laughter.

"You don't even know. This whole thing is The Librarian's fault. Crusty old dude promised to give dad some book then backed out on the deal."

"Your dad *kidnapped* me!"

"No he didn't!"

Randy was about to launch into a spirited

defense of his father's actions but decided against it. *Had* Douglas kidnapped her? That wasn't the right word, was it? His dad wasn't the kind of guy to abduct children. He coached Little League for crying out loud.

"He didn't kidnap you, Taylor."

"Really? Then why would I have to run?"

Randy didn't have an answer for that. The know-it-all had cornered him, just like know-it-alls love to do.

"I hope you haven't been up all night."

Taylor turned to find Douglas was watching from nearby.

"Who could sleep with you old men snoring?" she asked.

Douglas met Taylor's sneer with a smile. "Well," he began, "I hope you got a little rest. We're in for a long day."

Taylor was ready to respond when the raucous snore from inside the tent morphed into a coughing fit as someone new stirred from sleep.

"Smee," Hook said, "why have you let me sleep on like this when there's so much to do?" No one answered. "Smee! Wake up, you fool."

A muffled thud was quickly followed by a loud, "Yelp!"

"Get to your feet and let me out of this tent," Hook ordered.

"Yes, capt'n. Right away, capt'n!"

Smee stumbled from the tent and held its flaps wide so Captain Hook could step into the open.

Smee reminded Randy of an abused dog huddling at his master's feet.

"A battle on the horizon beats a sunrise every time. Wouldn't you say?"

"Yes, sir!"

Smee shoved his shirttails into his pants. When he took his spot beside Hook, the captain patted him on the back.

"Wake the men. The sooner we get moving the better."

"Aye!"

Hook's mate marched over to the clearing's edge and looked into the forest. "You heard the man. On your feet! Don't leave your captain a-waitin. Early to bed and early to rise. You scoundrels know the drill."

The woods came alive with the agitated moans of grown men being roused from sleep. Soon a diverse band of pirates began to file out of the forest and into the clearing. Some were pudgy, others bone-thin. Many smiled toothless grins, while a few had more teeth than their mouths could comfortably hold. A couple of the men wore eye patches to cover their most gruesome battle wounds, but most in the group proudly left their scars on display.

The kids watched as the Headless Horseman stepped from the shadows alongside the pirate horde, his orange eyes refusing to die like the campfire at their feet. Even when his hood was drawn, just one look at Bones was enough to send a chill the length of Randy's spine.

Randy looked around at the group he was traveling with, shaken to see how well his father fit in. Douglas was talking and laughing with the pirates like they were long lost friends, as if his dad were just another man in Hook's crew.

But Randy knew that wasn't true.

His dad would never take orders from someone like Hook.

If Douglas Stanford were a pirate he'd have a ship of his own.

Randy pushed the thought from his mind.

He didn't like the way that sounded either.

Not one bit.

CHAPTER 2

BACK IN OZ, The Librarian stood on the balcony watching the slaves who had congregated outside the Witch's castle. Moments before, the clouds had split to allow long pillars of light into parts of Oz that hadn't seen the sun in a very long time. The Winkies played in the sunlight like children in the year's first snowfall. Some made shadow puppets. Others ran and played tag. Many simply stared into the sky with arms outstretched, letting the sun bathe their weary bodies in warmth. It was a joyous time for those who had suffered under the Witch's reign.

But while the new sun signaled a brighter future for the people of Oz, The Librarian couldn't share their joy. Wesley had just revealed some terrible news. Hope had betrayed them, stealing the amulet he and Wesley would need if they wanted to return home.

The old man stroked the length of his beard. "Hope has worked in the library for years. It seems Douglas has been planning this for quite some time."

"Is there a way to get back without an amulet?"

Wesley asked.

The Librarian shook his head.

Wesley felt dizzy. Every success seemed to be immediately followed by an even greater failure. Sure, he'd led the slaves in a revolt against the Queen. But he'd done it all to save Tay – and now she was long gone.

"Wait. What about Locke?"

"Locke's a Lost Boy," The Librarian said.

"I know. But he was able to get into the library..."

"That's because he has an amulet of his own as Neverland's Watcher."

"So does Oz have a Watcher?"

The old man smiled. "That's where my thoughts were heading, too."

A wave of excitement pushed Wes forward a little faster. "That's it, right? We find the Watcher and use his amulet to get home. Boom! Problem solved."

Wes saw the old man didn't share his excitement.

"I don't understand. Why aren't you as pumped about this as I am?"

"The Watcher's home is a three-day hike from this castle. And that's if he's still there. I believe the Oz story is already correcting itself, but there's no way to know how long that will take. We could hike day-and-night only to discover he isn't there. For all we know, he's already gone back to Astoria to report what's happened here just as Locke did."

"So we're stuck?"

"Until the story corrects itself," The Librarian

said. "Yes, I believe so."

Wes closed his eyes, but it wasn't darkness that met him. Instead, he was back in the Witch's throne room, Taylor fading away to nothing before Wesley could reach her. It was a memory that had been playing on a loop ever since the fighting stopped. He couldn't get away from it.

Watching the boy, it seemed The Librarian could sense where Wesley's thoughts had gone. "If it helps, I don't think Douglas has any desire to hurt your friend. I imagine he only took her so she wasn't left behind in the chaos of the battle."

Wesley glared at him over the top of his glasses. "She wasn't going to be left behind. She was with me when a winged monkey flew away with her."

"I understand it's hard, but if we're patient—"

"There isn't time to be patient!"

The Librarian steeled himself against the boy's icy tone. "You'll have to be patient if you want a chance to save your friend. As much as we'd like to, we can't just click our heels together and wish our way back to Astoria."

Wesley shook his head in frustration. He turned away from the old man. But then something occurred to him that seemed to brighten his mood...

"Why not?" he asked. "Why can't we click our heels together?"

"Well, for starters, we don't have Dorothy's slippers..."

A sly grin split Wesley's face. "True," he said. "But I know where they are."

◆ ◆ ◆

Wesley and The Librarian found Dorothy's companions resting in the castle's throne room. With all of them together, Wesley shared the idea he'd already run past the old man. But when he was finished, he quickly realized his fairy-tale friends weren't as excited as he was. In fact, their only response was silence – that and a shudder Wes saw course through the Lion's body.

"It's wrong," the Scarecrow finally said. "We can't do that to Dorothy. She was a fine girl. This... it's just morbid."

The Tin Man nodded in agreement. So did the Lion beside him.

"We don't want to do it either," Wesley explained. "But what if this is our only way to get home? What if it's the only way to save Taylor? She's still alive, you know? I know Dorothy was your friend, but she's gone."

"I don't even want to th-think about it," the Lion said.

Wesley drew a frustrated breath. "Don't you want to give her a proper burial? We're burying the Witch's guards." He gestured to a nearby window. Looking out, the group saw the Winkies preparing to bury the battle's fallen soldiers in a rocky area across from the castle.

The Tin Man looked over at The Librarian. "You're okay with this?"

"Not at first. But there may be other reasons to excavate young Dorothy's grave. Even if the magic slippers don't help us, it would be wise to collect them so they don't fall into the wrong hands."

The companions considered this for a long moment; but still, none was ready to commit. Eventually, their silence became too much for Wesley to bear.

"I can't believe you guys!"

The group recoiled at Wesley's tone.

"Tay killed the Wicked Witch, and she did it for you. She saved everyone, and now you can't do this one little thing that might help us save her?"

"We want to help you," the Lion said. "It's just—"

Wesley cut him short. "You can only summon bravery to save yourself?"

Shame washed over the companions. Each averted his eyes so he wouldn't be the next to fall under Wesley's angry gaze.

Clanging a bit as he shuffled his feet, the Tin Man finally spoke. "You've done so much for us," he said. "We'll do what we can to help you."

The others slowly nodded in agreement, finally giving in as the Tin Man had. But while it was starting to look as if Wes and The Librarian would get their way, lines of worry creased the old man's brow. The boy was beginning to change. He was more confident now. Assertive. And there was something else. A defiance that felt all too familiar. It wasn't much. The others hadn't noticed at all. But it was enough to worry an old man...

An old man who didn't want to make any more mistakes than he already had.

◆ ◆ ◆

Ready to leave, Wes and The Librarian were hurrying down a stairwell when the first tremor hit. Wesley put his hand to the wall for balance, looking about as the floor wavered beneath his feet. He heard some high-pitched screams from downstairs, but they subsided a bit once the earth stopped moving.

"What the heck was that?" Wesley asked.

"I suspect things in Oz are beginning to shift back to the way they were originally written."

After waiting to make sure their footing was solid again, the two continued down the steps and started for the exit. When they came onto the castle's drawbridge they found news of their departure had traveled fast. A group of Winkies was waiting to see Wesley and his companions off.

Nell and the tinsmith were front and center in the crowd. Wesley wasn't surprised to see Nell verging on tears. She and Taylor had become fast friends. If word had gotten out that Wesley and the others were about to leave, Wes was sure everyone knew why they were in such a hurry to go.

"What happened to Tay?" Nell asked.

"We're not sure," Wesley explained. "We think someone took her away."

"The Witch?"

"No. The Witch is gone. You don't have to worry about her ever again."

"And now you're going to get the people who took Taylor..."

"We're definitely gonna try."

Nell nodded, but his answer had done little to comfort her.

Nell's father stepped forward. "You'll need help," he said. "We can be ready to leave within the hour."

Wesley shook his head. "There are too many people who still need help." He looked to The Librarian. "This is our fight."

Wesley shook the man's hand then started down the path with the old man. Just ahead of them, the Tin Man, the Scarecrow, and the Lion were already well on their way to the chiseled staircase that would lead them off the mountain.

As they went, everyone around them stopped what they were doing to watch the group depart. Some tried to hide their curiosity, while others were quite open, walking to the path's edge to bid Wesley and his friends farewell.

"I'll be glad when we're gone," Wesley whispered.

"Why do you say that?" The Librarian asked.

"Look at them. They're all looking at me like I'm some kind of freak."

The old man smiled. "It's admiration, Wesley. If Miss Taylor were here I'm sure they would be treating her the exact same way."

Wes heard concern in The Librarian's voice.

"You don't think it will work, do you?"

The old man leaned on his staff for support. "If you'd told me the boy I met in the library just a few days ago would lead the people of Oz in a revolt against the Wicked Witch of the West – I'm not sure I would have believed that either." He motioned toward the Witch's castle behind them. "You've given them a reason to believe you can do just about anything. Who am I to argue?"

The Librarian left Wesley to begin his descent of the treacherous staircase.

The stairs had intimidated Wes on the way up, but he'd stayed calm by refusing to look down. That wasn't an option now. They hadn't even started, but Wesley already felt like he was going to puke.

"Wesley!"

He turned to find young Nell had hurried down the path to offer her final goodbyes.

"Please be careful!"

Her voice was much stronger than it had been when they'd found her hiding beneath a table in her father's workshop.

"Tell Tay we love her!"

She waved goodbye. So did some of the others. A few applauded.

While uncomfortable with his new celebrity, Wesley forced a smile. The sendoff had boosted his confidence just enough to lessen his fear of the mountain he had to descend... and the unknown challenges waiting beyond.

CHAPTER 3

DOUGLAS LED HOOK'S crew on a hike through the woods that lasted most of the day. Randy and Tay were trailing behind the others with Hope and Smee when Hook moved closer to Douglas near the front.

"Are you sure you know where you're going?" Hook asked. The pirate had ditched his hat and coat in an effort to keep cool. It hadn't been enough. His shirt was stained with wet spots. His forehead shined, dripping sweat into his eyes.

"It shouldn't be much farther," Douglas explained.

"Ah! Splendid. That's good to hear. I'm fine, of course. But my crew, you see, they're... well... they're built for the high seas... not for a land-locked trek like this."

The pirate had brought nearly a dozen of his men. Each looked like he would pay a king's ransom to be back aboard the *Jolly Roger*. Most were red in the face from exertion. Several were so winded their breath was little more than a wheeze. Ironically, Hook was probably the worst of the bunch. He looked like he was ready to collapse on the spot.

"I guess it's a good thing we're here to enlist

some help," Douglas said.

"My men will be up to the task when the time comes."

"Good."

"I'm curious: how large is the army we're here to recruit?"

Douglas grinned. "Fifty-two strong."

"Fifty-two?"

"Think you can manage to have that many soldiers under your command?"

"What makes you think the Queen will grant you control of her army?"

"There's a monster in these parts known as the Jabberwock. No one's been able to kill it." Douglas tapped the gun in his waistband. "I'm going to help the Queen defeat her most challenging foe the same way I'm going to help you defeat Pan. When I have: you'll get your war."

A broad smile lit up the pirate's face. "Excellent."

"Seems like an awful fuss for a book," Smee said.

Hook glared at his mate for intruding on their conversation.

"It's not just any book," Douglas explained. "*The Manuscript* will give me a chance to control events in my world – a chance to make things right."

Hook furrowed his brow. "I don't understand: if your weapons haven't ensured your success in the real world, how can you guarantee they'll bring me success in my battle against Peter Pan?"

"I'm giving you a chance to rewrite your story," Douglas answered. "How well you do that is entirely up to you."

While Douglas was trying to soothe the pirate's concerns, his explanation only seemed to worry Hook more.

"Wait," he said. "Are you saying we'll still be controlled by words on the page? We'll still be fighting the same battles over-and-over again?"

Douglas stopped, blowing out a deep sigh as he turned to face the pirate. "All you've ever wanted is an honest chance to defeat the Lost Boys. That's what I'm giving you."

"I understand, but—"

A strange voice cut Hook short.

"*Hey!* Momma said *I* got to make the sandwiches."

Everyone looked into the forest. The tiny voice had come from somewhere just off the trail.

Still trailing behind the group, Taylor did her best to remain calm, but her heart was already racing.

"You made them last time," a second voice complained.

Douglas wheeled about. His gaze found Taylor just in time to watch as she threw a sharp elbow into Smee's side.

"*Watch out!*" Douglas screamed.

But Tay was already at it again. When she saw the first blow had been enough to double Smee over, Tay leapt into the air and brought her elbow down on the back of his head so he went face first into the dirt.

"Look, you idiots! Don't let her get away!"

Hook's crew scrambled to grab her, but it was too late.

Taylor had already disappeared into the woods.

◆ ◆ ◆

Already well off the trail, Tay weaved her way through the forest. She hadn't heard the voices since leaving the path, but knew whoever she had heard would have to be close by.

"Help! Please! They're right behind me!"

Taylor had used the element of surprise to get a head start on Hook's men, but now the pirates were right on top of her.

Tay hopped a fallen tree then stumbled into a small clearing where she slowed to a stop. "Hello," she whispered. "I know you're there."

"Is that Mary Ann?" a low voice asked from nearby.

"Be quiet, you!" an older voice scolded.

Taylor spun around. The squeaky voices seemed to be just a few feet away.

"I think it's the Alice child; the one from the flood."

"I said... shh!"

Taylor eased forward. "Please! I need your help!"

Tay stopped when she felt something crunch beneath the weight of her shoe. She could already tell it was something more substantial than a twig or a branch. Still, she couldn't believe what was waiting beneath her foot when she moved it aside.

Taylor had flattened a wicker picnic basket beneath the sole of her shoe. It sat atop a tiny, red blanket. Four white plates were placed at even intervals around the basket, each with a pile of large crumbs at its center.

"Hey! We were going to eat that!"

"I told you to be quiet!"

"But—"

The protesting voice ended in a muffle. Taylor was beginning to think the stifled voice belonged to a boy being reprimanded by his father.

Tay shifted her gaze from the dollhouse picnic to the trees just ahead of her. This time a slight movement drew her attention to some branches just overhead.

"What in the world?" Taylor exclaimed.

A family of four country mice stood together on the branch. Standing on their hind legs, three of the mice wore plaid pants with a vest to match. The other sported a short dress with shiny black shoes. One of the male mice had brass-rimmed spectacles perched on the end of his nose; his tiny face was punctuated by a crescent moon of grey hair at his chin. This older mouse had a hand over his son's mouth.

For a brief moment, Taylor felt her heart warm with wonder. It was the same feeling she'd had upon her arrival in Oz with Wesley and Locke; the same she'd felt when chasing those giant butterflies through the meadow. But then...

"This way," a raspy voice said. "I think she came

through here."

Douglas and Hook were coming through the trees just a few yards away.

There was no time to admire Wonderland's magic.

Taylor had to move.

❖ ❖ ❖

Douglas and Hook stepped into the clearing. Both scanned their surroundings.

"She couldn't have gone far," Douglas said. "She was right here."

Hook pulled his sword. "You can go back if you like. My men will find her."

Hook took a step toward the tree line, but Douglas stopped him with an outstretched hand. "Just wait," he said. "And put that thing away."

The captain didn't continue forward.

But he didn't sheathe his sword either.

Hook watched as Douglas fell to one knee.

"I think we may have interrupted someone's lunch. Take a look."

The pirate knelt beside Douglas, his eyes falling on the miniature picnic Taylor had discovered just a few moments before. "I'm beginning to believe this strange land you've brought me to is quite deserving of its name."

Randy stepped into the clearing behind them with Smee. Smee snorted laughter when he saw the disturbed picnic scene. "Guess they didn't have much of an appetite, huh?"

Hook smacked him with the back of his hand.

"I'm just sayin', capt'n."

"No one cares to hear your thoughts, Smee."

Ignoring them, Douglas rose to his feet and began to scan the area. The country mice had pulled together behind a trio of twisted branches. His gaze passed over them without notice, and all four breathed a quiet sigh of relief.

Hope swiped at cobwebs and dusted leaves from her sweater as she stepped into the clearing. "Anything?"

Douglas shook his head.

"I say let Wonderland have her, mouthy little thing that she is..."

"I'm not sure I'm ready to give up just yet. Besides, I think I may know someone who can help."

Before anyone understood exactly what that meant, Douglas lunged toward the mice so he caught them by surprise. Apparently, he'd seen them after all.

"Move!" Father Mouse screamed.

The tiny family scrambled for cover, each rushing for a hole in the tree's trunk near the end of the branch. All four hurried into the opening, but Douglas's hand shot through the gap right behind them.

His fingers wrapped around the youngest of the bunch. The boy's parents tried to pull their son from Douglas's iron grip, but all they could do is scratch and claw at Douglas's hand as he dragged their tiny son away.

Sporting a satisfied grin, Douglas held his captive into the air. The tiny mouse's head poked out from the top of his closed fist; its tail spiraled out from the bottom, lashing back and forth as the mouse struggled to break free.

"Look what we have here," Douglas said.

The mouse's family quickly reappeared at the end of the branch. "Please," the bearded mouse began, "we'll do whatever you want. Don't hurt my boy."

"It shouldn't come to that, but it isn't up to me. What happens to your son is in the hands of that little girl." Douglas looked past the clearing into the forest. "You've already ruined their picnic, Taylor. Don't make it any worse."

He'd raised his voice to make sure Tay would hear what was happening if she was still somewhere nearby. Truth be told, he didn't need to raise his voice at all. Crouched behind a fallen tree, Taylor was hidden not twenty yards away. She'd heard everything, including Douglas's threat.

"It's your call," he hollered. "One way or the other."

Tay scooted through the dirt, sure to stay close to the ground as she moved to get a better look. Meanwhile, Douglas tighten his grip.

"Dad?" Randy asked in a wavering tone. "Dad, what are you doing?"

"I'm not doing anything, Randal. Your friend's doing this."

The mouse gasped for air. His tiny eyes bulged in their sockets.

Mother Mouse screamed. Father Mouse grabbed acorns from the branch above them and chucked them at Douglas to no effect.

Randy rushed to his father's side. *"Dad! Stop! You're killing him!"*

But Douglas didn't listen. He just tightened his grip, his eyes darkened by hate. He ignored his son and the pleas from the mice. He was lost in a cloud, lost in a world of grey until Taylor's voice cut through the haze.

"Okay!" she said. "Stop! I'm coming out."

Everyone turned to watch as Taylor stepped back into the clearing.

"Let him go," she said somberly.

Douglas held her gaze, refusing to release the mouse.

"Dad?"

It was only at his son's prodding voice that Douglas finally shook from his trance and blinked his anger away. He loosened his grip, and the mouse jumped from his palm then scurried into the brush. Happy to see him free, his family quickly ran to join him.

"I can't believe you fell for that," Douglas chuckled.

Taylor smirked. "You know what's funny for real?"

"What's that?"

"Randy does the exact same thing."

His smile fell. "How so?"

"He always pretends like the whole thing was just a big joke."

Randy tried to intervene. "Shut up, Taylor."

"Does he threaten a lot of mice, my son?"

"Only if they're smaller than him."

Douglas reacted as if she'd socked him square in the gut.

Satisfied to know the blow had landed flush, Taylor brushed past them on her way back to the trail. "Don't worry, Mr. Stanford. I don't hate Randy nearly as much as I did five minutes ago. I finally see where he gets it."

CHAPTER 4

THE TIN MAN'S stiff joints made descending the mountain's steep staircase a chore, and the Scarecrow had to stop every few steps to coax the Lion along. Meanwhile, their slow pace had given Wesley and The Librarian ample opportunity to get ahead.

"I'm sorry for being such a jerk," Wesley said. "In the Witch's castle..."

"Sometimes I have to remind myself that you haven't taken the same vow I have. Just because your motivations differ from my own, that doesn't mean the stakes aren't just as high for you."

"What is Mr. Stanford after?"

The old man took a moment to weigh his answer. "The Elders call it *The Book of Real*. I... prefer *The Manuscript*."

The Librarian paused again and gestured toward the horizon. He didn't want Wesley to miss what lay before them. The thick mist that had clung to the mountain during their ascent had burned away in the morning sun. It left them with a view so beautiful no artist could capture its splendor. The two reveled in the scene for a moment; then the old man continued.

"Some believe *The Manuscript* will allow those

who possess it to control the real world just as an author can control one of his storybook lands."

"Seriously?"

The Librarian stopped on the next step. "Protecting *The Manuscript* will be just one of your many duties... if you're to become my apprentice."

Wesley's mouth dropped open.

"I've been the library's caretaker longer than you can imagine. I can't do it forever. My body is breaking down, and my mind isn't what it used to be."

"But I'm just a kid."

"So was I, if you can imagine." The old man leaned heavily on his staff as he moved to the next step. "But it's as a child our imagination is its most robust. It's only as a child that you can learn to harness the power of your creativity; but it's only with discipline and dedication that you can learn to control it."

Wesley didn't move. "Randy's dad was your apprentice, wasn't he?"

The Librarian answered with a sad little grin. Of course, all that did was beg Wesley to question The Librarian further. He was about to do just that when the ground wavered beneath their feet.

"Earthquake!" the Scarecrow yelled.

The Tin Man nearly toppled over. The Lion cowered, hiding his face behind his large paws as debris dropped down on them in a curtain of dust and gravel. Above them, the grinding of stone was so loud Wesley thought the entire mountain might come down on top of them.

If they fell to their deaths, at least they'd get a proper burial.

In the end, the companions didn't fall.

But the mountain did...

A wave of jagged rock and stone tumbled toward them.

"Avalanche!" The Librarian yelled. *"Move!"*

All five scrambled down the steps. It took all they could manage to keep from falling. The staircase shimmied back-and-forth with such force it felt like it might slide out from under them.

Wesley came to an abrupt halt. The others nearly knocked him over on their way down.

"What are you doing?" The Lion whined. *"G-go!"*

Stones pelted them from above, the first of many if they didn't find cover.

Wesley looked about. Debris clouded his vision, but he spotted a rocky overhang a short distance from the stairs. It would provide just enough cover if they could make it.

"Look!" Wesley shouted. *"There!"*

Without a second thought, the Scarecrow took a running leap for the ledge. He barely made it, nearly falling into a deep crevasse before finding his balance. When he was safe beneath the ledge, he turned to help his friends.

The Tin Man tried to get the Lion moving, but the Lion was already cowering again with his tail between his legs. *"Lion, please! Get up! Hurry!"*

Wesley put a hand to the Tin Man's back and

guided him toward the enclave. The Scarecrow was there to help, grabbing the Tin Man's hands to help him stay balanced as he stiff-legged his way to safety.

Once the Tin Man was secure, Wesley fell to both knees beside the Lion. *"C'mon! Let's go!"* Wes could barely hear his own voice over the deafening roar of the avalanche. Even if the Lion had heard, he didn't listen. Wesley tugged on the Lion's mane but it wasn't enough. The beast wouldn't move.

"Look out!" the Scarecrow yelled.

Wesley looked up just in time to see several mammoth boulders tumbling down on them. No time to escape, Wes threw himself onto the ground beside the trembling Lion, covering his face with his arm as he braced for impact...

But it was an impact that never came.

Too scared to look, Wesley could hear the avalanche all around them, two freight trains rocketing past on either side. And yet, he and the Lion hadn't been buried in debris. In fact, Wesley's back wasn't being pelted with rocks anymore either.

The boy looked up to see The Librarian was standing just a few feet away with his weathered staff held high into the air. The stone atop his staff was emitting a yellow light that had taken the shape of a giant dome. While transparent, the dome blocked any debris that came toward them. Dirt slid down its sides. Rocks bounced off it. When a large boulder plunged toward them, Wesley cowered again, sure the magic barricade would buckle beneath the force of its impact. But the dome held true. Like everything else, the dome directed the boulder away from them and down the side of the mountain.

The Librarian grimaced as if keeping the dome in place was a great burden, but Wes was in awe of what the wily wizard had done. Even after everything they'd been through, Wesley had never seen The Librarian in this light; he'd never understood the power that came with being the library's caretaker...

A power The Librarian wished to bestow upon him.

CHAPTER 5

TAYLOR NOTICED THE group had tightened up around her to make sure she couldn't escape again. They weren't making it too obvious, but Tay could tell Hook's men weren't thrilled to know a little girl had gotten the jump on them. They were ready to pounce if she tried again. Meanwhile, Hook didn't seem to mind so much. He was walking alongside Douglas and Smee, the trio trailing behind Bones as the hooded figure cleared the path of brush and limbs with his sword.

They had walked in silence for nearly an hour when Taylor found herself flanked on either side by Hope and Randy.

"You aren't as smart as you think," Hope finally said.

"What's that supposed to mean?" Taylor asked.

"What you said back there. You think you know him. You don't."

"I know enough. I know I'm a little version of my mom, and I know Wesley's dad is the best kind of geek. And I know no one is born a bully. They have to learn it somewhere."

Tay was sure to let her gaze fall on Randy as she finished her statement. All Randy could do in response was look away.

"Everything is so simple when you're twelve-years-old," Hope sneered.

"I don't even know what that means."

"Why did *you* come back to the library? You and Wesley?"

Taylor looked down at the dirt. It was the first time she didn't have a rapid-fire response ready to launch back at her. "You know why I came."

"Does Randy? Does he know the two of you are responsible for evil taking over in Oz? That Dorothy died because of you? Does he know the real world will be different when he finally gets home?"

"You're wrong. We killed the Witch. Things will go back to normal."

"You *hope* they will."

"I don't understand," Randy said. "Why would changes in Oz have any effect in the real world?"

Hope allowed Taylor to answer.

"All the worlds are connected," she explained. "We changed the story in Oz. When we got home, everyone thought Dorothy was the bad guy. There was no Hollywood movie, no *Over the Rainbow*. Everything was different."

"But that's not why you came back," Hope reminded.

"Wesley's life didn't change much, but *Wizard of Oz* was my favorite book. For me, living in a world without the book I knew made a huge difference. People talked about me like I was some kind of thug. Teachers hated me. Caleb Rodriguez thought we were best friends. I went from the honor roll to barely passing. We changed history in Oz, and it wrecked my life in the real world."

Randy shook his head. "That's impossible. Teachers love you so much it makes my stomach hurt. And Caleb would never—"

Taylor cut him off. "He treated me like I was you."

Randy was stunned.

"And what about your dad?" Hope asked.

Sadness washed over Tay. That awful morning in the kitchen with her father felt so distant it might as well have been from another life. In a way, it had been.

"The way he looked at me, the way he talked. You could tell… you could tell he hated me like everyone else."

She expected to find a satisfied grin on Hope's face, but it wasn't there. Instead, Hope smoothed a circle on Tay's back to comfort her. Taylor wanted to pull away, but she couldn't bring herself to do it. After replaying the episode with her dad, she was desperate to have her feelings soothed.

"I'm sorry," Randy said. "That… sucks."

"It could have been worse," Hope explained.

Taylor's head snapped up. "Really? How?"

"What if he didn't recognize you at all?" Hope allowed the question to hang in the air a moment. "Your life went a little sideways. Five minutes later you're breaking and entering. But what if it had been worse? What if you lost your father completely? How far would you go to get him back?"

Taylor flashed a crooked grin. "He's the only family I've got. I feel sorry for anyone who tries to take him away from me."

"And if it takes thirty years to get him back?"

"Then it takes thirty years."

Randy looked toward the front of the group with a furrowed brow. His dad was still walking with Hook and Smee. The three men were just out of earshot so they couldn't hear what was being discussed behind them.

"Dad says he's known The Librarian since he was our age."

"He has," Hope said.

This time it was Taylor shaking her head in frustration. "So what's the point?"

"That you aren't the first to have their life ruined by the library's magic. Once upon a time, Douglas was The Librarian's apprentice. But when *he* came back from the storybooks lands, it was like he had never existed at all. His parents didn't recognize him. Neither did his friends. He'd been erased from existence."

Taylor's expression softened a bit. "What happened?"

"The Elders wouldn't let The Librarian use *The Manuscript* to help Douglas. Instead, they sent a twelve-year-old boy into the world to fend for himself."

Taylor shook her head in disbelief. "I don't

believe you."

Hope smiled, but it wasn't a mean-spirited look. Just one that suggested Hope knew it would take Taylor a little longer to accept the truth about Douglas.

"Even if I did," Taylor continued, "that doesn't excuse what he's done."

"What do you mean?"

"I watched him torture The Librarian. He's stolen from people. He's attacked innocent strangers who have nothing to do with this. And yes," she shot her eyes at Randy, "he kidnapped me."

"So?" Hope asked.

"He can't treat people that way because something bad happened to him!"

"But it's too late to say that, Taylor. You already told us there's *nothing* you wouldn't do to regain your family if you lost them. Guess what? The man you're convinced is such a bad guy – he feels the exact same way."

Randy gave Taylor a chance to respond before taking the conversation down a different path. "There's something I don't understand," he said.

"What's that?"

"Dad thinks he can use *The Manuscript* to get his old life back?"

"That's the plan."

"What happens to the life he's built?"

"What do you mean?"

"Tay's life was turned upside down because her

favorite book got a new ending. What going to happen when dad rewrites the last thirty years?"

This time Hope was the one drawing a blank.

"I'm sure he's got that figured out, Randy. You'll have to ask him."

With that, Hope quickened her pace to put some distance between herself and the children. She'd given them enough to think about.

❖ ❖ ❖

The Queen's castle was far more inviting than the Witch's lair in Oz. Made of shimmering white stone, the castle sat on beautifully manicured grounds populated by bright flowerbeds and cool fountains. As they approached, it was impossible to miss all the features shaped like hearts: windows, doors, the archway over the entrance... a thousand details to please the Queen.

A narrow field of rose bushes sat between the forest and the castle's gate. Most of the flowers were red, but white blooms dotted some of the green shrubs. Not that they would for long. Two gardeners were working furiously to paint the white roses red as Douglas and his group approached.

Not that these were ordinary gardeners...

"Well," Smee began, "that's 48omething you don't see everyday."

With no previous knowledge of Wonderland, the pirates couldn't believe their eyes. The gardeners were shaped like oversized playing cards. Their bodies were oblong, no thicker at any point than a heavy piece of cardboard. Randy remembered the figures from the Disney film, but there was something about the way their appendages seemed to spring from nowhere that made his stomach lurch.

Animated was one thing, living and breathing was something else.

"You've gotten paint on the ground," the Six of Spades snarled.

"I don't know what you're complaining about," the Two shouted. "I may have spilled a little paint, but you got red on one of my pips. That'll never come off."

The Two scrubbed at a splash of paint that had partially covered one of the spades on his chest.

"Maybe the Queen will confuse you for a member of the royal family."

"Great," the Two smirked. "I'll have the Queen screaming in my ear all day."

Suddenly worried someone might overhear, the Six looked about with concern. "Don't talk like that around me. I'll lose my head just for listening to you."

"That won't happen," the Two scoffed.

"I got two words for you: Friends of Alice."

The Two scrunched up his face. "That's three words, you idiot."

His companion counted on his fingers to make sure the Two was right. "You... you know what I mean! Besides—"

"*Hello there!*"

The cards looked up to see Douglas and the others approaching. They immediately dropped their brushes and pails. Both grabbed shovels and prepared to swing at anyone who stepped their way.

Douglas threw his hands into the air. "Wait! We aren't here to fight."

The Two gestured with his shovel to the pirates. "Coulda fooled me, traveling with that lot."

"I promise we aren't looking for a confrontation. We're friends if you'll allow us to be. We support Her Highness. We're seeking an audience with the Queen."

Looking unsure, the Two dropped his shoulders and cocked his head in confusion. "You want to meet the Queen?"

Douglas nodded.

"You aren't afraid?"

Randy's dad offered another silent response.

The Two looked to his companion for guidance. "What do you suppose we do? No one's ever *asked* to see the Queen."

"Are you daft?" the Six barked. "We send them on their way! I won't be the one to interrupt her day. Besides," the Six jabbed his shovel towards Tay, "that one looks just like Alice."

"I promise to accept full responsibility if the Queen is upset by our presence."

"You're talking as if the Queen sees reason." The

Six leaned forward so he could be heard while speaking in a lowered voice. "She's quite mad, you know?"

Douglas didn't respond.

"No," the Six said. "No, no. I won't do it. Be on your way!"

The Six turned away from them to pick up his bucket of paint. While unsure that he should, the Two did the same.

Randy saw Douglas had moved his hand so it was poised to pull his gun.

"Dad," Randy whispered. "Don't."

"We have to get past them, Randal."

"So? Is that the only way you know how to handle things?"

Douglas stepped away from his son. "What else am I supposed to do?"

"I don't know. Just," he gestured to the gun, "anything but that."

After a moment's thought, Douglas turned his attention to the playing-card men once more. "One moment," he said.

Neither of the cards was happy to hear the conversation would continue.

"You said no one has ever come to visit the Queen?"

"People know better," the Six explained. "I'm surprised you don't. Unless you're an outsider. If you're an outsider I shouldn't be talking to you in the first place!"

"But don't you think she'll be upset to learn

you've turned her only visitors away? You're making decisions for her. I may be an outsider, but I know she won't be happy about that."

The Six lifted his shovel, ready to swing. "Unless we kill the lot of you, leave no one to tell the tale. You won't have me be the next to lose his head."

Taylor and Hope traded a nervous look. The pirates stiffened, and Hook pulled his sword.

"I suggest you try it, thin man. My crew can easily handle the two of you."

The Two spun his shovel so it was pointed at Hook.

Douglas quickly stepped between them.

"Stop! It doesn't have to go that way." He fired a cold look at Hook before making one last attempt to reason with the playing-card men. "Listen: if she gets angry we'll tell her that we forced you to take us inside. She'll believe that."

The Two shifted his attention to the wrought-iron fence that bordered the rose garden. A drawbridge had been lowered just beyond the gate to allow people across the moat that circled the Queen's castle. "What do you think, Six?"

Douglas answered before the Six could.

"It's more than fair," he said. "You can't lose."

The Six started toward the Queen's castle and gestured for Douglas and his group to follow. "You say that now. As bloody as the Queen's been of late, it wouldn't surprise me if we've all lost our heads by the time she's through."

CHAPTER 6

WESLEY AND HIS companions found a place to rest after they reached the base of the Witch's mountain. While his fairy-tale friends sat beneath a shade tree, Wesley stood with The Librarian in the afternoon sun. He'd taken the old man's staff and was pointing it at a pile of stones the two had collected. The boy's discouraged look was enough to reveal that whatever he was supposed to be doing wasn't working... not one bit.

Eventually, Wes lowered the staff to his side. "I don't understand why you can't just teach me one of your spells."

"Because that magic is meant for me," the old man explained. "Baum was the only one who could create this land, just as Wonderland could only spring from the mind of Lewis Carroll. You must tap into *your* creativity if you're to succeed."

"So I'm just supposed to stand here and pretend I can do what you do until it works? That doesn't make any sense."

"Not what *I* do," The Librarian explained. "I grew up reading tales of Merlin; I fell in love with Tolkein's Gandalf. When it was time for me to craft my own magic, it looked very much like theirs. But that doesn't mean yours will look the same. What inspires you? When I tell you that your creativity is your only limit, what do you imagine yourself doing?"

Wesley wasn't surprised to hear the old man took his inspiration from a character like Merlin. He'd come to think of The Librarian as a wizard from another age. And yet, Wesley struggled to think of a specific character *he* could latch onto in the same way. After all, when he stayed up late with a flashlight and a book he never found himself longing to be one of the *characters*.

"What if my inspiration is completely different than yours?" Wesley asked.

"That's what I'm telling you. It should be different."

"That's not what I mean. I don't want to be Harry Potter. I want to be J.K. Rowling. I like Ray Bradbury, Stephen King, Brian K. Vaughan... guys like that."

Wes thought he saw a flash of concern in the old man's eyes.

"Those are authors, Wesley."

"So? When you're inspired by Merlin, you're limited to the types of magic Merlin can use. If you're inspired by Tolkein: you can do anything."

The Librarian sighed. "Let's focus on the stones."

Wesley's shoulders slumped into a frown. He looked over at the others. They tried to avert their eyes, but it was clear Wesley and The Librarian had their full attention. "Fine," he said. "I'll try."

"Don't try. If you believe you're an author, think

about the stories you write. The stories you write for yourself that no one else will see. Are they easier to write than the essays you pen in English class for your teacher?"

Wesley laughed. "God yes!"

"And why do you think that is?"

"I know it sounds crazy, but I just let the story do its thing. The characters take over. I don't even think about it. It just happens."

"Not just. When you write those stories you've freed yourself of your inhibitions. That's when we are our best selves. That's what you must do here."

Wesley responded with a nod then lifted the staff. He didn't want to try again, not in front of the others, but he knew there was no getting out of it, not if he was to become The Librarian's apprentice.

Wesley spun the staff until the canary-colored crystal was pointed at the pile of rocks once more. He closed his eyes, trying hard to do just as the old man instructed – to let go of his inhibitions, to stop thinking so hard, to just be.

But was that even possible? So much had happened. Things had gone so badly since he and Tay first stepped into Oz. It was all he could think about. The Librarian was asking him to clear his mind as the world crumbled around him. Frustrated, Wesley quietly wished he was back in his room, a book in his hand and his phone on silent. That was his happiest place. There was nothing in the world he enjoyed more...

The comforting image was only in his mind for a

few moments when Wes felt a charge of energy surge from the staff into his hands. It felt warm and powerfully electric, as if the energy could empower him to fight armies of men – or consume him so he dropped dead on the spot. The staff no longer felt like a carved piece of wood in his hand. It was part of him. Wes and the staff were one. He could throw its energy just as easily as he could throw his fist; it could be controlled like any other part of him.

Doing his best to remain calm, Wesley reached out with the charge. He felt it envelope the stone atop the pile and lift it into the air.

The Librarian's eyes widened as he watched from nearby. The Tin Man and Lion shared looks of surprise as the Scarecrow bounced to his feet.

Wesley's eyes remained closed, but everyone else was watching.

Each saw it for what it was...

The boy's first steps in learning to control the library's magic.

"You're doing it, Wesley!" the Scarecrow exclaimed. *"You're really doing it!"*

That was all it took. Wesley's eyes popped open, and the rock fell into the dirt.

The Scarecrow looked down at his feet. "Oh... sorry."

Embarrassed, Wesley shoved the staff toward The Librarian. "This is stupid," he said. "I'm not you. I look like an idiot playing make believe in his room."

The Librarian shook his head as he took the staff

from Wesley. "Kids your age are always so interested in how they look to others."

Wesley saw the old man's disappointment, but it only served to intensify his anger. Wes was about to lash out further when—

"Hey! Look there!"

Everyone glanced over to see something in the valley below had stolen the Lion's attention. They hurried over to join him.

"What's happening?" he asked.

The sun had risen above the mountain so it was now bathing the valley in its warmth. As sunlight moved across the landscape, everything it touched came alive. Dead grass slowly turned green. Wilted flowers began to bloom. Even the bubbling brook that twisted through the valley's floor seemed to turn a brighter shade of blue. The sun was like a natural paint brush bringing color to a drab canvas. Life was returning to Oz just as they had hoped it would. It wouldn't be long before it had stretched from Winkie Country to Munchkin Land. And yet, The Librarian didn't react the way Wesley thought he might...

"Oil your joints, Tin Man. We'll need to move faster than I originally thought."

"What's wrong?" Wesley asked. "It's just the reset, right? The story's correcting itself like we thought it would."

"That's what I'm afraid of..."

❖ ❖ ❖

The Librarian led Wesley and the others as they continued their trek across Oz. They hadn't stopped to rest in some time, and Wesley found it strange The Librarian refused to discuss his new sense of urgency.

Most of the day had passed when the Lion and the Scarecrow brought the group to a halt on a barren hillside.

"I think this is it," the Scarecrow said.

"Oh no," the Lion murmured.

"What's wrong?" Wesley asked.

"The straw we used to mark Dorothy's grave: it's gone. It must have blown away in the wind."

Not only had the wind removed the straw from Dorothy's grave, it had scrubbed a good deal of loose dirt from the hillside so its face was smooth and uniform. The grave's markings were gone as were any telltale signs of disturbed earth that might have helped them locate the site of her burial.

Wesley shot an angry look at the Lion. "Why would you use straw to mark her grave?" He pointed to the Scarecrow. "He doesn't know any better, but you..."

The Lion cowered just enough to make Wesley regret his sharp tone.

None of this was the Lion's fault.

Wes rubbed the Lion's head to let him know he wasn't really mad before turning to face The Librarian. "So that's out. How do we get home now?"

"I'm afraid I can't be too concerned with our own predicament," The Librarian explained.

"Why not?"

"All day we've watched life return to Oz. If the winds of change can bring flowers and trees back from the dead..."

The Lion sat down. "You mean, Dorothy... she might die all over again?"

"If she springs to life like everything else? I'm afraid it's possible, yes."

The Tin Man leaned on his sledgehammer. "How terrible."

The group stood in silence for a long moment, no one sure what to say or do until–

"Oh no!" the Scarecrow shouted. "Look!"

Just as they'd witnessed in the valley earlier that day, the group watched as life returned to the hillside in a wave of color. The grass and flowers under their feet would spring to life in a matter of moments.

As would anything buried in the dirt beneath them.

"Oh, Dorothy!" the Scarecrow exclaimed. *"Poor, poor Dorothy!"*

The transformation continued across the valley, touching each of the rolling hills around them. Wesley tried to push the ghastly thought from his mind, but he couldn't stop imagining what it would be like to wake up beneath a pile of immovable earth. The dark vision sent a shock of ice splintering up his spine, consuming him so his own breath caught in his chest. He stood there, unable to breathe until something caught his eye.

"Oh god," Wesley muttered.

The adjacent hill was coming back to life just like the one they were standing on – with one notable difference. The nearby hill had an imperfection on its face about six feet long: a strange, oblong mound of dirt. The mound was without grass or flowers as if the earth had been disturbed in this one spot.

"We're in the wrong place!"

Wesley darted down the hillside. The others spotted Dorothy's grave then took off after him. The Librarian and the Tin Man fell behind, but the Scarecrow kept pace with Wesley while the Lion raced ahead on all fours.

But even as Wesley sprinted down the hill, he knew it wouldn't matter.

It would take him several minutes to make it to Dorothy's grave. If she'd come back to life with everything else, Wesley and his friends would never make it in time.

❖ ❖ ❖

Wes and the others had already cleared about a foot of earth away from Dorothy's grave when The Librarian arrived with the Tin Man.

"Hey!" the Scarecrow said excitedly. *"Hey! I've got something!"*

Wesley glanced over to see the Scarecrow had

excavated the top half of Dorothy's silver slippers.

But her feet weren't moving.

"Hurry!" The Librarian said. *"Clear the dirt away from her face!"*

Wesley did just that but instinctively recoiled when Dorothy finally appeared. She was a pretty girl, her hair done in two pigtails tied with blue ribbon to match her checkered dress. But her skin was grey like an overcast day. Her neck and face were covered with swollen bee stings.

The Lion grabbed Dorothy's arm and dragged her lifeless body from the shallow grave. The Librarian quickly handed his staff to Wesley and knelt beside her. Taking a quick measure of the girl's chest, he began forcefully pressing down on her breastbone with the heel of his hand.

"What's he doing?" the Scarecrow asked. His tone bordered on accusatorial.

"CPR," Wesley explained. "He's trying to bring her back."

The Librarian finished his first set of chest compressions then blew several breaths into Dorothy's lungs...

Nothing happened.

The others couldn't watch, but Wesley kept his gaze fixed on The Librarian as he worked for more than ten minutes to bring Dorothy back.

Ten chest compressions followed by two deep breaths. The same thing, over and over, until The Librarian looked like he would collapse from exhaustion.

In the end, it just wasn't enough. There was nothing he could do.

Winded, the old man rose to his feet. "I'm so sorry," he said.

"This is all my fault," the Scarecrow explained. "It was my idea to mark her grave with straw. If only we'd used rocks..."

"It wouldn't have mattered," the Tinman explained. "We weren't even looking in the right place."

"But we would have *known* that."

The Lion looked up at the old man. "Do you really think she w-woke up beneath all that d-dirt? I c-can't even imagine how scary that would be."

"Let's assume some things are too permanent for magic to erase."

Wesley trudged over to Dorothy's lifeless body. While everyone's heart ached, his hurt for a different reason. For Wes, the possibility of Dorothy's resurrection meant something more. Part of him thought that if she came back, if they were able to breath life into Dorothy, that meant anything was possible...

There was a chance to get home.

There was a chance to save Tay.

There was a chance for life to look normal again.

Wesley closed his eyes and leaned on The Librarian's staff. He felt stupid for getting his hopes up. Only *Oz* author L. Frank Baum could bring Dorothy back, and he'd been dead since before Wesley was born.

All at once Wesley felt a swell of energy enter his body through the staff. The surge was so unexpected and intense that his muscles seized. His arm hairs stood on end. Unlike before, Wesley couldn't hold onto the magic. It was too powerful to contain, like trying to catch a lightning storm in his hands. Besides, when his eyes finally opened to see what was happening–

So did Dorothy Gale's.

The young girl at Wesley's feet bolted into a seated position and gasped for air. The sparkle of her blue eyes was enough to light up her face. It wasn't long before a blush brought color to her cheeks and pushed the clouds away.

Her fairy-tale friends rushed to her side, but The Librarian went straight for Wesley. "What happened? What did you do?"

"Nothing," Wesley said. "I swear."

Dorothy's welts vanish before their eyes – there one minute, gone the next.

"Where am I?" she asked in a daze. Her attention fell on the Scarecrow, and her eyes widened. "It's you. Oh goodness. For a second, I was beginning to think this was all a dream."

No one knew how to respond. When a barking dog appeared from the brush and started toward them, they didn't have to say a word.

"Oh, Toto! Toto, where have you been?"

Toto leapt into Dorothy's arms and licked her face.

"Easy now," the Scarecrow said. "She's been

through a lot."

Toto yapped a complaint, and everyone laughed – everyone but the old man.

The Librarian took his staff from Wesley as the others helped Dorothy to her feet. Like everyone, he assumed the library's magic had taken a little longer to bring Dorothy back. It made sense. Breathing life into plants was one thing. Resurrecting a human life was something else. Still, The Librarian couldn't help but wonder if Wesley had somehow brought Dorothy back on his own.

"I see you've made some friends," Dorothy said.

Wesley offered his hand and introduced himself. The Librarian joined them so he could do the same.

If only he'd taken a moment to study his staff he might have noticed there was evidence to support his theory about Wesley...

The pale crystal atop The Librarian's staff was no longer yellow.

It was grey.

CHAPTER 7

THE PLAYING-CARD SOLDIERS did not take them into the castle. Instead, they forced Douglas and the others into a tiny building near the dense forest that bordered the property.

"This isn't good," Taylor whispered to Randy as they entered.

"What are you talking about? Why not?"

"Why would they bring us into the courthouse?"

Long benches lined either side of a red carpet guiding them toward the front of the room. When they reached the carpet's end, Randy noticed a group of strange creatures and exotic birds cordoned off in a separate seating area. Each of them had a slate chalkboard perched on his lap.

Randy motioned toward them. "Let me guess: that's the jury?"

"Which makes her the Judge."

Taylor directed Randy's attention to the woman waiting impatiently behind a wooden bench just ahead of them. She sat on an elevated throne that allowed her to look down on those present. Her face was caked with white makeup. Her lips gave the impression they were in a constant pucker because she had applied lipstick in the shape of a red heart. Strangely, her head seemed just a smite big for her body – and her gold crown a touch small for her head.

"What is this?" the Queen finally asked. "Who are these people?"

The Six of Spades popped his heels together. "They say they've come a great distance to meet you, your Majesty."

"Really?" The Queen considered Douglas for a second then fluffed her hair. "Have them take a seat. Today's hearing shouldn't take more than a moment."

The Six gestured to the benches. Douglas and his companions took a seat in the front row. Hook and the others sat in the bench directly behind them.

"Do you know what's going on, captain?" Smee asked.

"Only that I'm beginning to grow impatient," Hook said.

"Let's get this over with," the Queen said. "Send in the accused."

The giant doors at the back of the room swung open. Sunlight streamed into the building from outside, backlighting those in the doorway so it was impossible to make out their features. And yet, both prisoners were easily recognizable in silhouette, even to outsiders like Randy and Tay.

"Oh my god," Taylor gasped. "It's the Mad Hatter. The Hatter and the Hare."

The guards prodded the prisoners along. The Hatter walked so quickly the Hare had to double-time his hops to keep pace.

Remarkably, the Hatter looked very much like the character the kids knew from the Disney film. He had paired a tuxedo jacket with a giant bow tie covered in polka dots. Yellow hair puffed out on either side of his head, the rest of it hidden beneath a rumpled top hat. A white tag had been secured within the hatband with a note that read, *In this style: 10/6.*

When the pair reached the front of the room, the Queen leaned forward for a better look at the Hatter. "Didn't we sentence this one once before? I do believe he's the one who murdered my time."

At this, a new member of the court appeared. Shuffling into view, the White Rabbit hustled up a slanted staircase until he was standing behind a podium near the Queen's bench. He wore a fine silk vest that offered a pop of color in the otherwise dingy room. The chain of a pocket watch hung in an arc from his hip before disappearing into the pocket of his pleated pants.

"I asked you a question, Rabbit."

Whiskers twitching, the White Rabbit cleared his throat as he prepared to read from a scroll of yellowed parchment. "Yes, your Great, that appears to be correct. The Hatter was, in fact, sentenced for murdering time."

"Yet he's still walking around with that pretty, little head."

Oblivious, the Hatter blushed like she'd meant it as a compliment.

"He seems to have escaped execution. But I'm afraid these two have been brought before the court on new charges today. Serious charges. They're thought to be... Friends of Alice."

The jury gasped.

"What do you have to say for yourself?" the Queen asked coldly.

"Well, your Majesty—"

"Take off your hat when addressing the court."

"Oh," the Hatter began, "this isn't mine."

"Stolen!"

The Queen's booming voice was nearly enough to make the Hatter jump out of his skin. "No, no! You don't understand. I sell the hats. They don't belong to me. I'm a Hatter, you see." He looked down at the March Hare beside him, the grey rabbit slurping tea like he couldn't be bothered with the events unfolding around him. "I believe we've had this conversation before. Don't you?"

"Take it off!" the Queen demanded.

He quickly removed the hat and clutched it against his chest.

The Queen smiled. She looked like a predator baring its teeth before descending on its prey. "Very good. Now... proceed."

"All I did was help Alice to find her muchness," the Hatter explained. "Would you rather me be a bad host? We were celebrating my unbirthday, and Alice happened upon us at exactly six o'clock. It was time for tea."

The Hatter's buck-toothed friend responded to this with great concern.

"I'm worried we'll be late for today's tea," the March Hare explained.

He showed the court his teacup was now empty. As he presented the cup, the Hatter pulled a pocket watch from his pants and popped it open. Upon seeing the time, he became a bundle of nervous energy, suddenly bouncing back and forth from one foot to the next. "Oh dear! Oh dear! My furry friend is correct. We have to get back before we're too late."

The Hatter stepped to leave, but two guards lowered their spears to block his path.

"Whether you sit for tea again will depend on your sentence, Hatter." The Queen shifted her attention to the Hare. "What say you on the matter of Alice?"

"I have nothing to add," the Hare explained.

"Nothing?"

"Nothing at all..."

"Be sure to write that down," the Queen instructed. "It's very important."

The jury feverishly scrawled notes onto their slates. All but one. Randy noticed a lizard in the jury box was barely paying attention at all. Instead, he was following a fly with his eyes, mouth open like he was ready to snatch it out of the air with his tongue.

"Freakin weird," Randy said.

The words were barely off his lips when the jurors looked up at Randy in unison. Then each of them added something new to their slates. Two words...

Freakin weird.

"This is even crazier than I remember," Taylor said. "It's completely unfair."

Hope nudged the children. "Stay quiet, you two."

The kids stayed silent as the hearing continued.

"Well," the Queen began, "I'd say we have enough evidence to continue."

The White Rabbit nodded excitedly. "Oh yes, your Majesty. More evidence than we need, to be honest."

"Then it's time for my favorite part."

"The verdict?"

"No," the Queen answered. "Sentence first."

"Very well. What is your—"

"Off with their heads!"

The March Hare leapt into the air. His hair stood on end.

"Oh dear!" the Hatter exclaimed. "How will I showcase my hats without a head to place them on?"

"Take them away! Both of them! They can die with the other conspirators when the sun sets tomorrow evening."

Guards descended on the Hatter and the Hare. Two of them took hold of the Hatter, each grabbing one of his arms so they could lead him away.

Another took hold of the Hare by his floppy ears and lifted him into the air, intent on carrying him to the door just like that.

Taylor had had a hard enough time staying quiet through the trial. But watching them haul the Hare away in such cruel fashion was finally too much...

"You can't treat him like that! Put him down!"

The court members gasped at Tay's fiery tone.

"Excuse me?" the Queen asked with bewilderment.

Taylor pushed to her feet. "I don't care what he's done. How would you like it if someone carried *you* around by the ears?"

"I'm the Queen of Hearts. No one would dare!"

"Because it would hurt?"

"Yes," the Queen screeched. "It looks excruciating!"

"Well, you should treat people the way you want to be treated."

The Queen pinched her brow in a look of confusion. "That may be the *dumbest* thing I have *ever* heard."

"Dumber than this trial?" Taylor asked. "How can you hand down a sentence without a verdict? What happens if you find out they're innocent?"

Giggles and snorts echoed through the courthouse.

"Oh child, they wouldn't be here if they were innocent."

"But how do you know? What proof do you have?"

"The proof will be presented at their trial," the White Rabbit explained.

"*After* you've cut off their heads?"

"Precisely."

Growing impatient, the Queen sighed. "What's your name, girl?"

"Taylor..."

"Are you sure? You remind me of the Alice child..."

"I think I know my own name."

"You might, but you might not. In my kingdom, if I say your name is Alice then your name is Alice. My voice is the loudest. I sit on the throne. It's my opinion that matters. Which means if I say you're guilty... *then you're guilty!*"

Taylor shrank back into her seat beside Randy. The Queen's high-pitched screech had been enough to make her teeth hurt.

"Good job," Randy muttered.

Tay jabbed a sharp elbow into the boy's side.

The Queen began cooling herself with a paper fan printed with red hearts. "Let's get on with it," she said. "I don't like talking to the girl, and you know I get sad when forced to spend too much time with common folk like this. What have these people been charged with today?"

Douglas quickly rose from the bench before the Rabbit could answer. "If I could, you Majesty, we aren't here to be sentenced."

"Then why are you here?"

"Well," Douglas stammered, "I'm... I'm the King of Astoria."

Hope and Tay nearly choked, but Randy was all smiles.

"I'm the King of Astoria, and I'm here to save your kingdom."

CHAPTER 8

BACK IN OZ, Dorothy's friends filled her in on recent events. Not wanting to upset her, they were sensitive enough to gloss over the details of her demise. They told her that she'd fallen ill after being stung by the Black Bees and that they'd gone on to kill the Witch without her. Of course, they'd made some friends along the way… like the Tin Woodsman.

The sun was nearing the horizon when Wesley found himself walking with Dorothy. She smiled at him then gestured to the Tin Man who was walking with the others just ahead of them. "I've never seen a man made of metal before."

"It takes some getting used to," Wesley said.

The two walked in silence for a few moments.

"So you're stuck in Oz like me?" Dorothy asked.

Wesley nodded.

"Did a twister suck you into the sky? That's what happened to me."

Wesley looked at his feet. "No, we managed to get stuck here all on our own."

"The others said something about a girl…"

Wesley couldn't hold back his smile. "Taylor. Yeah. She's my best friend."

"Where is she now?" Dorothy regretted the

question when she noticed Wesley's discomfort. "I'm sorry. I didn't mean to pry."

"No. It's just... she was taken by some bad people. That's all we know, really."

"She means a great deal to you, doesn't she?"

This question made Wes more uncomfortable than the last. Kids at school liked to joke about his relationship with Tay, making it sound romantic when it had never been. The jokes usually ended with Taylor pushing some loud-mouthed kid into the dirt, which was good because it meant Wesley never had to admit the truth...

He'd always had a crush on Taylor Morales.

"Does she feel the same about you?" Dorothy asked.

"No," Wesley said without hesitation. "She doesn't look at me like that."

"It must have been hard to hear that from someone you care about so much."

"Well, she's never been mean enough to say it."

Dorothy looked perplexed. "Then how do you know?"

"I just... I do... guys like me never end up with the girl."

"I don't understand. What kind of boy are you?"

Wesley shrugged.

"I think you should ask this girl how she feels," Dorothy said. "I wouldn't want some boy assuming something like that about me. What if he's wrong? I might spend all my days waiting for him to court me."

Wesley nodded in agreement, but he already knew he wasn't going to take her advice. Finding the courage to fight fairy-tale villains was easy compared to storming the castle they were talking about now.

The Scarecrow came bouncing over toward them. "We're there! We made it!"

The meadow outside the Tin Man's cabin was flush with freshly bloomed flowers. The Tin Man sat down on a nearby stump, his metal face showing just enough emotion the others could see something was wrong.

"Are you okay?" the Scarecrow asked.

"I have a great many memories from my time here," the Tin Man explained. "Returning is... bittersweet."

Dorothy took in their surroundings. "We walked right by this spot on our way to see the Wizard." She looked over at the Scarecrow. "Do you remember? Before we happened upon the Lion in the woods."

"I do," the Scarecrow began. "I do remember! I'm not sure I've ever remembered something more than a few hours old. Oh! What a feeling!"

"Get used to it: the Wizard's promised you a brain when we get back."

"Hey! I remember that, too!"

While it wasn't his home, the cabin brought back memories for Wesley too. From its doorway he had watched Taylor chase those giant butterflies through the meadow. Not only that, it had been just outside that door where he'd stood up to Randy Stanford for the first time – the way Taylor always told him he could.

The old man inspected the cabin's entrance.

"So," Wesley began, "we're here. What now?"

"Your guess is as good as mine," the old man explained.

"I thought you said we could open the portal home once we had Dorothy."

"Our amulets are forged from the same material as the slippers, but that doesn't mean they'll work the same way. It doesn't mean they'll work at all."

"So what are we going to do?"

Dorothy joined them before The Librarian could answer. "Is there anything we can do to help?"

"Well," The Librarian began, "we're not really sure. We were hoping..."

The old man's voice trailed off when something at their feet stole his attention.

Dorothy followed his gaze. "Oh my!" she exclaimed. "What's happening?"

Dorothy's slippers had sparkled in the sun for most of their journey, but now they were aglow in a cloud of tiny, blue lightning bolts.

The others quickly took notice.

"D-Dorothy," the Lion stuttered, "what's happening to your shoes?"

"I don't know!"

"Oh, man!" Wesley exclaimed. "Look!"

The cabin's entrance had come alive just like Dorothy's shoes. The door's wooden frame seemed to snap and pop with electricity as the doorway filled with shimmering light that reflected their images back to them.

"What's happening?" the Tin Man asked.

"It worked," The Librarian said matter-of-factly. "We've found our way home." He turned to face Wesley. "I'm afraid we won't have time for long goodbyes."

Wes nodded to let the old man know he understood. Then The Librarian smiled at the group and carefully started through the portal. When he pushed through, the portal's light swirled around him like water whirling around someone gliding into a lake.

"That's it?" the Scarecrow asked. "You're leaving just like that."

Wesley's fairy-tale companions were already grouped in a tight semi-circle around him. He'd been so focused on getting home, he'd never taken time to think that this would be the last time he'd see them... his friends.

Locke had known the perfect thing to say to Wesley before returning to Neverland. Wes wanted to impart some piece of wisdom that would help guide them on the journey ahead of them, but he couldn't think of anything to say.

"Are you sure we can't go with you?" the Lion asked. "We could help you to save Miss Taylor the way she helped you save us."

A tilted grin split Wesley's face. "And they call you cowardly."

The Lion looked away to hide his prideful smile.

"Thank you," the Scarecrow said. "For saving us. For making things right."

"For everything," the Tin Man added.

The three of them turned away so Dorothy could step in to say her goodbye. While the others had been looking at Wesley, her gaze was fixed on the portal behind him. "Could I use that to get back to Kansas?"

"I think you still have a little work to do here," Wesley said.

"It isn't fair. We've only just met. I think we would have been friends."

The Tin Man pointed to something behind Wesley. "Look!"

Tentacles of light coiled outward from inside the portal.

"Oh my!" Dorothy exclaimed.

"It's okay," Wesley said. "You guys get going."

"You're s-sure?"

"If you hurry, you'll make it to Emerald City before dark. Besides," Wesley said. "I really can't bring myself to say goodbye."

While reluctant, Dorothy and her friends turned to start their journey toward Emerald City. The orange sun was just low enough that they appeared to be walking into the sunset. It was enough to warm Wesley's heart, forcing a smile to his lips as the portal's tentacles wrapped around his slight frame and pulled him through to the other side.

CHAPTER 9

AFTER DISMISSING HER court, the Queen of Hearts suggested she and Douglas talk over a game of croquet.

"It's a game for royalty," she had said. "Don't you agree?"

As they made their way onto the lawn, Randy was troubled by what awaited them. Like everyone else, he knew how the game was played in Wonderland. But reading about Wonderland's version of croquet was one thing...

Seeing it in real life was something else.

In person, the game seemed downright cruel.

Two guards wheeled a metal cage onto the field. Half a dozen terrified flamingos were crammed into the tiny entrapment. All of them flapped about nervously as the Queen approached. Ignoring their fits of fear, the Queen reached into the cage and grabbed one by its throat. She yanked it free with such disregard the flamingo banged its head against one of the metal bars.

"Choose your mallet wisely," the Queen said.

While hesitant to follow her lead, Douglas eased his hand into the cage. He did everything he could to avoid hurting the birds, but the flamingos fought back, swatting and pecking at his hand until

Douglas was forced to be just as aggressive with his choice as the Queen had been with hers. He pulled it from the cage, wrapping both hands around the flamingo's neck until it fell into submission.

"Dad!" Randy shouted. "Be careful."

"Can I assume you know how the game is played?" the Queen asked.

"I do," Douglas responded. "And I'll warn you: I'm pretty good."

"We'll see about that..."

The Queen dragged her flamingo by its wiry legs so its head dragged in the grass behind her. A guard was waiting with the White Rabbit near the field's empty grandstands. He held a tiny hedgehog on each of his outstretched palms. Each of the bristly critters had its head tucked between its hind legs so it formed a tight ball with prickly skin.

The Queen snatched one of the frightened animals. Just as hesitant as before, Douglas carefully took the other.

"It's been some time since you've had a playing partner, your Majesty," the White Rabbit said. "I'll be rooting for you."

The Queen fired a cold look at the Rabbit until he cowered behind the guard's leg. "Set the field," she said.

The guard bowed his head. "Very well, your Majesty. *Set the field!*"

Near the end of the lawn, a squad of playing-card soldiers had been standing at attention. Upon hearing the order, the soldiers sprang into action, scattering across the courtyard. After reaching their assigned spots, they immediately dropped to their hands and knees. Then, each bowed his paper-thin body until it formed a perfect arch. Just like that, there were a dozen goals scattered across the lawn.

The Queen dropped her hedgehog onto the grass then turned to look at Douglas. "As a guest in my kingdom, I think it's only right that you go... *second.*"

Grinning, Douglas stepped back so he was standing with Hope and Randy. Hook and the pirates prepared to watch the game with great interest. Hook, in particular, wasn't sure what to make of all this.

"Smee, have you ever seen anything like this?" Hook asked.

"No sir, capt'n. There's a lot going on around here we don't see in Neverland, I think."

Ignoring everything but the game at hand, the Queen flipped her flamingo so she was able to hold it by the ankles. The bird immediately set its body so it was pin-straight and rigid. The Queen lowered the flamingo until its head was directly behind the waiting hedgehog. Then, after carefully checking her aim, she pulled the flamingo-mallet back and—

THWUMP!

She was lucky to make contact with the hedgehog-ball at all.

The hedgehog squirted off her mallet, rolling head-over-heels through the grass on a path that would ensure it came nowhere near its intended target.

But something unexpected happened as the ball rolled across the lawn. Unexpected to the pirates, at least. Those from the real world had a good idea what was about to happen: the Queen's subjects were going to help her win.

The playing-card man who had formed the wicket she was aiming for quickly crawled through the grass until he was situated in the ball's path. He came to rest just in time for the ball to pass beneath him.

The Queen's subjects erupted into applause.

So did Smee.

"She is pretty good. Huh, capt'n?"

Hook rolled his eyes.

"Your turn," the Queen explained.

Douglas awkwardly took hold of his flamingo. He addressed the ball, lowering the flamingo's head behind the hedgehog at his feet. "I'm so sorry about this," he whispered. "Truly."

THWUMP!

He didn't strike his ball nearly as hard as the Queen had struck hers. But what Douglas lacked in power, he made up in accuracy. Somehow his first attempt was rolling straight for its mark. It was just about to pass beneath the playing-card hoop when—

The soldier in that position scooted aside so the hedgehog rolled past.

It wasn't enough that the Queen's subjects were

going to help her score.

They were going to ensure Douglas didn't.

The Queen grinned. "Better luck next time, friend."

At their feet, the White Rabbit could barely contain his laughter. "He'll need more than luck, your Majesty. That was the worst shot I've ever seen!"

This was how much of the next hour went.

No matter how bad her aim, the Queen's shots seemed to find their marks. Meanwhile, Douglas couldn't pass his ball through any of the hoops. Not that he cared much. Sure, the Queen was cheating – but he wasn't there to beat her in croquet. He was there because he needed the Queen's help...

Just as he'd told the Witch in Oz and Hook in Neverland, Douglas explained he was on a quest to recover a magic book and that he was hoping to enlist her help. "In return," he said. "I can offer you weapons that will help you to defeat the one thing in Wonderland that hasn't fallen under your rule – the Jabberwock."

Barely listening, the Queen fired her final shot across the field. With a little help from her men, this one hit its intended target like all the rest. The crowd erupted in applause, and the Queen curtsied to acknowledge their adoration.

"Tell me," the Queen began, "these magic books in your land. Did they predict you would lose so badly today?"

Douglas forced a laugh. "No, your Majesty, I don't think there's any magic in the world that could have predicted I would lose *this* badly."

"Yes, well, we've had a good deal of fun, but I'm afraid it has to end here. I'm sorry to say my men won't be able to help you on your quest."

Douglas looked about in confusion. "I don't think you understand."

Anger colored the Queen's pale cheeks red. "You want to take control of my playing-card army, don't you?"

"Yes, but—"

"Then I understand just fine!"

She handed her flamingo-mallet to one of the guards then smoothed her dress with both hands.

"My men have pressing matters to attend to. They can't leave to help you."

Most of the soldiers present were still on their hands and knees, straining to keep their backs arched after more than an hour. Douglas wanted to point out that these men didn't seem to be doing anything too important but decided against it.

"It's my mistake," he said. "Maybe I wasn't clear. The books in my world have a funny way of predicting the future, and I worry that one day your kingdom will be destroyed by forces you aren't prepared to face. Don't allow your destiny to be controlled by words on a page. The storybook lands may be caught in endless loops where you live the same days over-and-over again, but that doesn't mean we shouldn't work to make sure the story is written in your favor."

"Have your books told you the story of Alice?" the Queen asked.

"They have..."

"Then you know she invaded my kingdom. She brought nothing but havoc on her little stroll through my lands. Then, in her most egregious act, she had the audacity to insult me in front of my subjects. She's disappeared from Wonderland, but my men will find her. Until they do, we are rounding up anyone who befriended that nasty child during her stay. The Friends of Alice will lose their heads, then my men will bring me Alice so that she loses hers."

"Aren't you worried about the Jabberwock?"

"That monster hasn't come down from the mountain in years."

"But what happens when it does? Your people have trusted you to protect them. Don't you want to know their trust has been earned. Help me now and I can give you the weapons you need to dispatch the Jabberwock with ease. I can give you the tools to protect your people."

The Queen picked at her fingernails. "I'll be honest. I don't care for my people much. Some of them look so strange. And the way they talk. I hate what I can't understand. No, I'm far more concerned with the girl who embarrassed me. Anything else can wait."

Hook chuckled from nearby, amused to hear the Queen talk so bluntly.

For his part, Douglas didn't know what to say.

But Taylor did.

"Can we go back to what you said before? Are you really going to *execute* people because they were nice to a stranger?"

"Of course," the Queen answered. "If you don't punish such behavior, what's to deter people from doing the same in the future? It can't be allowed."

"But aren't you being nice to a stranger now?"

The Queen squinted her eyes. "I don't like talking to you very much."

Taylor shifted her attention from the Queen to Hook then back again. "You should," she said. "You should love me. I'm the only one from my world who will tell you the truth about what's really going on."

Hope tried to intervene. "Be quiet!"

Tay didn't listen. "He's told you guys so much about the books that control your worlds – don't either of you want to know what those books are called?"

Hook and the Queen looked to one another, confused.

"Isn't that a funny detail to leave out?" Taylor asked.

Hook stepped forward. "The book details my war with Peter Pan. I never gave the title much thought."

The Queen shook her head in frustration. "You're making my ears hurt, young lady. Come to your point or get off of the field."

Douglas tried to grab hold of Taylor before she could say any more. "She doesn't have a point. She's just a little girl who—"

"Neverland's book is named after Pan."

The news staggered Hook.

Taylor whipped around to the Queen. "Yours is called *Alice in Wonderland*."

The Queen was stunned as well.

"A book about *my* kingdom is named after Alice?"

"I don't understand," Hook stammered. "Why would these books be named after the children?"

"Because people love Alice and Peter. In our world – they're the heroes."

"That's enough," Douglas snarled.

The group turned silent for a long moment.

Hook looked like he needed to sit down.

"What does this book say about me?" the Queen asked.

Taylor smirked. "That you're a villain just like him. You're not very good at it either. You're there to entertain kids like me. We laugh at you. We laugh when Alice gets away. It's the best part."

The White Rabbit began hopping around at the Queen's feet.

"Friend of Alice! *Friend of Alice! It's in her eyes! Friend of Alice!*"

"I told you before," Taylor began. "I'm not a

Friend of Alice. I'm like everyone else in my world...
I'm a fan!"

The Queen's eyes widened. She took in a deep
breath – so deep her head swelled, jowls trembling.
She held the air in her lungs until it seeped out of
her ears in stretched clouds of grey steam. *"OFF...
WITH... HER... HEAD!"*

Still in their positions for croquet, the playing-
card soldiers snapped their heads around so they
could see what was happening.

*"Did you hear me? Kill the Fan of Alice! Off with her
head!"*

Her men sprang to their feet. Two rushed over
and seized Tay, each grabbing one of her arms.

"Should we throw her in the dungeon with the
others, your Majesty?"

Without warning, the Queen stepped forward
and smacked the soldier with the back of her hand.
"If that girl's blood hasn't spilled in the next few
minutes you'll be waiting for the Joker's axe right
beside her."

The Queen's men began escorting Taylor off the
field.

"Bring out the executioners! Bring me the Jokers!"

Randy watched in horror as the soldiers dragged
Taylor away. He couldn't understand why Tay
wasn't doing everything she could to fight them off.
Even worse, he couldn't believe his father hadn't
spoken up to help her. His dad just stood there
watching with everyone else.

"Dad," Randy prodded, "we can't let them take

her."

Randy could tell his dad was trying to decide how to handle things, but they didn't have time to be strategic.

"What are you doing? Stop them!"

"What is that boy of yours saying?" the Queen asked. "I don't like his tone."

Randy looked across the lawn. It was only then that he realized the soldiers were escorting Taylor to a tall, wooden platform at the end of the field. A large block sat on the raised stand, a half-moon cutout featured prominently on its uppermost edge. Randy's stomach flipped.

It was the executioner's platform, and that was the chopping block.

It was where those who crossed the Queen went to die.

This was really happening.

Adrenaline surged through the boy until he felt like he was going to shoot out of his shoes. Instead, he sprinted onto the playing field without saying a word.

The move caught everyone off guard, including his father.

"Randal! Don't!"

"What is he doing?" the Queen screamed. *"Stop him! Grab the boy!"*

Playing-card soldiers sprinted after Randy. Two nearly caught him, but he dropped to the ground and slid through the grass, cleanly evading them so the soldiers collided into one another.

Randy scooped up one of the hedgehogs as he bounced to his feet. He turned to find the remaining men marching toward him with their weapons drawn.

Without thinking, Randy hurled the hedgehog in their direction. Eyes bulging, the animal curled in on itself so it was nothing more than a spiked ball. Squealing, it nailed the first soldier square in his chest. The blow was enough to send the soldier careening back so the whole group of them went down like bowling pins.

"Don't you do this to me," the Queen muttered. "Not again. Not like before."

Randy spun around just in time to see the soldiers escorting Taylor had turned to confront him.

"This is the end of the line, boy. Stand down."

Randy lowered his shoulder and barreled over him. He sent the soldier toppling back so he landed on his back in the grass. From there, Randy pinned the soldier beneath his foot and ripped the spear from his hands. He wheeled about and swung the spear in a wild arc.

"Duck!"

Taylor dropped, allowing the spear to pass over her head. The spear caught the remaining guard in his chest. The blow sent him flying. For a moment, he seemed to defy gravity, swaying back and forth in the air like a dropped piece of paper floating back to earth.

Randy hurried over to Taylor's side. "You

alright?"

"What are you doing?"

"We're getting out of here!"

"What? I'm not going anywhere with you!"

A spear whistled through the air between them, narrowly missing both children. The kids turned to find most of the Queen's soldiers had recovered and were now storming their way.

"You can hate me later!"

Randy grabbed Tay's hand before she had a chance to protest further. He nearly yanked her off her feet as he started for the tree line.

The Queen continued her rant. *"Hurry, you fools! Before they get away! I want them both! Kill the girl! Kill the boy! Off with their heads!"*

At this Douglas blinked out of his trance, directing his attention to the Queen across from him. "Wait! That's my son out there!"

But there was no getting through to her. The Queen was in a blind rage. It would take more than talk to bring her out of it. But there was no time for that. Instead, Douglas looked over at Bones and saw his flaming eyes were burning bright beneath his dark hood.

"Bring me my son. And be sure to punish anyone who gets in your way."

CHAPTER 10

RANDY HAD EASILY dismantled the Queen's soldiers on the playing field, but evading them in the forest was proving to be more of a challenge.

Their thin bodies allowed them to slide in and out of the trees. They grabbed onto branches when they could, using the added leverage to propel their bodies forward. The thin men seemed to sail through the air from one tree to the next. Their feet never touched the ground.

"Are you seeing this?" Taylor asked.

"I see 'em!"

Randy's legs burned. Beside him, Taylor was running low on juice, too.

"Well, you got us into this. What are we gonna do?"

"*I* got us into this?"

The kids sprinted down a steep grade that bought them a few moments of cover. When Randy stopped, Taylor plowed into him at full speed and nearly knocked him over. "What are you doing?" she exclaimed.

Scanning the area, Randy's attention fell on a mammoth tree at the center of a clearing just a few yards away. A massive hole in its trunk had grown so large the tree was completely hollow at its base.

"There," Randy said. "Fast!"

Randy hurried toward the tree. Taylor followed close behind him.

When they arrived, Taylor saw the tree's hollow offered just enough room for both of the children to squeeze inside. Randy gestured for Tay to slide in first. "Go ahead."

"You're sure?" Taylor asked.

There was a rustle of movement on the hill above them, treetops swaying back and forth as the soldiers closed in.

"I'm sure we won't outrun those things," Randy said. "It's now or never, girl."

"Don't call me girl!"

"Whatever! Are we doing this?"

Tay eased her way into the tree's hollow then shoved over so there was room for Randy to join her. It was a tight squeeze, but it was all they had: their last hope of escape. The playing-card soldiers would either pass without seeing, or the kids would be trapped...

They'd know in a few minutes either way.

❖ ❖ ❖

Two soldiers stalked through a meadow just a few yards away from the tree where the children were hiding.

"I don't like this," one of the soldiers explained. "We shouldn't be here."

"What are you talking about?" his companion

asked.

"We're walking through the Dark Woods."

"Let me guess: the Jabberwock?"

"It's the only thing that scares me more than the Queen."

"Everyone knows the Jabberwock's been living atop the mountain these last few years. As long as we stay beneath the tree line we'll be fine."

Still inside the tree, Taylor inched forward for a better look. She could tell the soldiers were closing in. All she wanted was to get a sense of how close they might be.

Instead, two birds fluttered into the air from the foliage at their feet. Tay batted at them with an open hand, letting out a little yelp of surprise when the birds went flying out of the hollow.

She slapped a hand over her mouth. She'd done enough to give their position away if the Queen's men had been within earshot.

Randy looked into the clearing to find the soldiers were out of sight.

"Are they gone?" Taylor whispered.

Before Randy could answer, a spear pierced the tree's trunk. It cut right between them, so close if either of the children had taken a step in the other's direction it would have ripped a hole through them just as it had torn through the tree.

This time there was no reason for Taylor to stifle her scream.

The unseen soldier pulled the spear free. Randy grabbed Tay, yanking her to cover just as the spear jutted into the hollow once more. Its arrowhead tip sliced Randy's arm on its second pass before being pulled free once more.

In and out, over and over, the spear came at them from every angle. It missed more often than it hit, but it wasn't long before Randy and Tay both had several jagged cuts on their arms and legs where the spear had made just enough contact to break the skin.

And then the second soldier made things worse...

As the first soldier continued to pierce the tree with his spear, the second buried his axe in the tree's massive trunk.

"What is that?" Taylor hollered.

"He's gonna cut the tree down if we don't come out!"

The soldiers took turns. The first would push his spear into the hollow, then the other would swing his axe in an effort to chop down the tree.

Randy screamed when the axe blade cut a slice in his back. Taylor immediately wrapped an arm around him to make sure he was okay.

"We have to get out of here!" Randy exclaimed.

"We can't outrun them!"

"They've already caught us, Tay!"

Randy crouched down like he was about to sprint through the hollow's entrance. Taylor tightened her ponytail then positioned herself as well. But before either could make their move...

The soldiers' efforts came to an abrupt halt.

"Wh-what's happening?" Taylor asked nervously.

Ignoring her, Randy listened for any clue of what was going on outside. A murmur passed between the guards then—

"Oh God! Wh-what is th-that?!"

"I told you!" one of the soldiers shouted. *"The Jabberwock!"*

Randy and Tay listened with clenched teeth as the soldiers tried to fight off the unseen horror. Metal clashed on metal. A flash of flame passed through their vision. Occasionally, the kids got a brief glimpse of the attacker: a cloud of smoke that seemed to pulse with life and move however it saw fit.

When the battle was done, all they heard were the last, agonizing breaths of the Queen's men. Then the cloud of smoke materialized in the tree's entry.

Both kids breathed a sigh of relief when the haze came together in the shape of a figure they recognized. The Jabberwock hadn't come out of hiding to dispatch the Queen's men...

It was Bones.

❖ ❖ ❖

The Headless Horseman reached into the tree's hollow before either of the kids had a chance to react. His powerful grip found Randy's leg. Desperate, Randy reached for vines hanging from overhead. When he fell to his stomach, he tried digging his fingers into the dirt.

Terrified, Taylor watched the Horseman drag Randy away. She reached for Randy when it was clear he wouldn't be able to escape on his own. But it was too late. Randy was gone. So was Bones.

Tay inched out of the tree's hollow. She ignored the bodies at her feet, instead scanning the area in hopes she would catch a glimpse of the Horseman and Randy before they disappeared. While she didn't see either of them, Tay could hear Randy cursing up a storm from somewhere beyond the trees.

Taylor looked toward Randy's voice then shifted her gaze in the opposite direction. Bones had not come for her, and he'd been good enough to take care of the soldiers who had before grabbing Randy. She'd gotten the help she was after. She was free. All she had to do was turn and go the other way.

❖ ❖ ❖

Bones carried Randy over his shoulder on his way back to the castle. Randy pounded Bones with his fists. He did his best to knee his captor in the chest. But his efforts to break free had little to no effect.

Eventually, Randy gave in and stopped trying to fight the brute off.

"Okay," he said. "You can put me down! I'm not going to run!"

Ever silent, Bones did not answer.

"Did you hear me? I said I'll go with you."

Again, there was no response from Bones.

Then someone new broke the silence. *"Hey!"*

Confused by the new voice, Randy strained for a better look.

Taylor had caught them. She was standing atop a large boulder near a waterfall he and Bones had passed just a few moments before. Randy was stunned by the sight of her. It wasn't the way she was standing atop that rock: so defiant and strong. It wasn't that she seemed confident to face off against the Horseman. It wasn't even that she'd come to help him...

Taylor was carrying the fallen soldier's axe.

Bones turned around so Randy could no longer see.

"There're two ways we can do this," Taylor explained. "What's it going to be?"

The Horseman threw Randy into the gravel beside him. Then a cloud of grey smoke materialized around Bones, swirling like a tiny tornado before taking the shape of a sword in his right hand. They were both armed now. The only difference: the Horseman's weapon was alive with orange flame.

Taylor gulped. " Okay? So maybe there are a few other ways."

She hopped down from the boulder and started toward them.

"Dude," Randy began, "what are you doing? I'm fine. Just go!"

Bones stepped toward her, his eyes burning hot with rage.

It was only as the pair closed on one another that Randy realized he was now completely out of the Horseman's line-of-sight. He rose to his feet just as Bones lunged at Taylor with his fiery sword raised.

Taylor gripped the axe with both hands. The Horseman was just about to bring his weapon down on Tay when—

Randy pelted him with a large stone.

Catching Bones off guard, the blow was just enough to shift his balance so Taylor could block his fiery blade.

Even the glancing blow was nearly enough to knock Tay off her feet.

She backed away just as Bones took another swipe at her. Then another. Taylor backpedaled as quickly as she could, eventually falling when the rocky footing became too difficult to manage.

Luckily, that's just when another of Randy's rocks caught Bones in the head.

The stone punched a hole in the Horseman's pumpkin flesh. He wailed in pain, flame spouting from the wound. Enraged, Bones turned about-face and charged at Randy.

Eyes wide, Randy chucked one stone after another. Most bounced off their attacker's chest like pebbles on a boulder.

But then one of the rocks found its mark and ripped a hole in their attacker's face.

"Again!" Taylor shouted. *"Again!"*

The next was large enough to take the Horseman's head clean off his shoulders. This quickly brought the attack to a halt. Bones fought to get his balance. Then he bent at the waist, feeling along the ground in search of his skull.

"What now?" Randy asked.

"You really have to ask?"

Sensing they were about to flee, Bones began swinging his flaming sword in wild swoops, desperately hoping one of the blind attempts would take care of the children. Randy and Tay fell to their backsides to prevent being cut in half. Once on the ground, both stayed silent so they wouldn't give themselves away.

Bones continued forward with his maniacal attack, staggering about blindly and swinging his sword until he finally connected with something: the waterfall.

The water extinguished the sword's flame in an instant. When it did, the weapon morphed into a long tendril of black smoke and disappeared on the wind.

Bones fell to his knees. Somewhere nearby, his Jack-O-Lantern head howled in agony.

"Oh my god," Taylor murmured. "That's it: his head."

She looked over just in time to see the fallen Jack-O-Lantern head pivot to look at her. Its eyes turned to angry slits.

"Randy! Get his head! Throw it in the water!"

"What?"

"Hurry!" Taylor shouted. *"Do it! Do it! Do it!"*

Randy sprang to his feet. He reached for the Horseman's head only to pull away when the Jack-O-Lantern tried to bite his hand.

"You grab his head!" Randy argued.

Taylor couldn't answer. Bones had zeroed in on her location and was now charging at her full steam. Without his weapon, the Horseman was ready to kill Tay with his bare hands.

Seeing she was in trouble, Randy kicked the Jack-O-Lantern over so its face was in the dirt then grabbed it with both hands.

A few feet away, Bones threw himself on Taylor and wrapped both hands around her throat.

"Akk!" Taylor choked. *"Do...iT..."*

Randy reeled back and threw the pumpkin head as hard as he could toward the waterfall. It left a trail of smoke hanging in the air behind it. Flame trailed the head like a missile until it passed through the water and the fire went out for good. When it did, Taylor's ghastly attacker transformed into a black cloud of smoke. The cloud maintained the form of a headless man for a few moments, his wispy fingers still wrapped around Tay's throat. But then the apparition began to dissipate with the wind. A moment after that, it was gone. Two kids from Ms. Easton's sixth grade English class had done what the people of Sleepy Hollow never could: they'd bested the Headless Horseman.

INTERLUDE

TWELVE-YEAR-OLD DOUGLAS STANFORD was sitting alone in The Librarian's office. He'd been there for hours, but he'd been locked away in the building for much longer than that. It had been several days since he'd returned home to discover his life had been erased from existence.

The boy was just about to nod off when the old man entered the room.

Douglas bounced to his feet. "Well," he said excitedly. "What did they say?"

Looking solemn, The Librarian shook his head.

Douglas nearly burst into tears on the spot. "What? Why?"

The old man took a seat on a long bench in the corner. He motioned for young Douglas to do the same. "The Elders feel it's too dangerous. They don't want to risk additional changes in the storybook lands."

"Why would that even happen?"

"You have to remember: no one's ever used *The Manuscript*. We don't know what might happen once we've unleashed its power."

"Okay? So what? What am I supposed to do?"

The Librarian sighed. "The Elders have suggested we... well..."

Douglas furrowed his brow. The old man could barely get through his answer.

"The Elders have suggested we take you to a group home..."

Douglas shot to his feet. "An orphanage?!"

"Temporarily, Douglas. Just for the time being."

The boy turned to hide his face.

"And maybe it never comes to that," the old man explained. "We still have a few days. It's Friday now, you and I can spend the weekend scouring books together. We'll find what's changed then..."

"Then?" Randy scowled.

The Librarian looked up from the bench with sad eyes.

He didn't have an answer for that.

Anger swelled within Douglas. He finally understood why the Elders had refused to meet him face-to-face. It's a lot easier to do something like this when you haven't familiarized yourself with the victim.

"At least my parents didn't do it on purpose."

"Douglas—"

The boy cut him off. "And we don't need the weekend. If you're going to throw me out like a piece of trash let's just get it over with."

The Librarian quickly got to his feet when the boy started for the door.

"It's the middle of the night."

"I'm sure that's when most kids get abandoned on their doorstep."

"Douglas, please... we... we can't just give up."

The boy stopped in the doorway, turning to look back at his mentor. "You gave up the minute you let them do this to me."

CHAPTER 11

CAPTAIN HOOK FOUND the adult Douglas standing near the tree line with Hope. He was just staring into the forest, his attention fixed on the spot where Randy had disappeared into the woods with Tay.

"My men are ready," Hook explained. "What would you have us do?"

Lost in thought, Douglas didn't respond.

"I'll be honest," the pirate continued, "I think it's in all children to get in the way of our plans. I'm sure there's some point to their existence, but I couldn't tell you what it is. Every child I've met is nothing but trouble. I'll tell my men to go after them posthaste."

Hook started to leave, but Douglas grabbed him before he could.

"You'll do nothing of the sort," Douglas snarled through his teeth.

Hook looked over, incensed to discover several of his men were there to witness the exchange.

Douglas bit at his lip before continuing. "You're here to do what I tell you, captain. Nothing more. When I tell you to put your sword away, I expect you to do it. Otherwise, you can return to your pathetic existence in Neverland. Are we clear?"

Hook kept his black eyes on Douglas for a long moment. "We're clear," he said. "Now take your hands off of me."

Douglas gave the pirate a little shake before finally letting him go. When he did, Douglas turned toward the ruckus building around the Queen.

"I want that girl!" the Queen screamed. "Hunt her down! I want her back on this field before the day is out. The boy, too. They'll both see the executioner for their insolence. I demand it as your Queen! Bring me the children. Off with—"

A deafening gunshot cut the Queen's order short.

The soldiers cowered. Hook's men reached for their swords.

Still standing near the tree line, Hook saw Douglas had taken the pistol from his jacket. He was holding it in the air, a wispy curl of smoke rising from its barrel.

"I've heard enough," Douglas said coolly.

Everyone stared in disbelief. Smee was the only one who seemed to be enchanted by the weapon in Douglas's hand. "A canon you carry 'round in your pocket. Oh! Pan will never see that one comin, capt'n?"

Douglas stepped forward. The Queen flinched beneath his icy gaze, sure he was going to hit her.

"That boy is my son," Douglas said. "Do you understand? My flesh and blood. If anything happens to him, I'll hold *you* responsible."

"But... but I'm the Queen of Hearts..."

"That may be. But if my boy's hurt I won't stop

until Wonderland's been wiped from the map. Do you understand? If it goes that way, when I'm finished there won't be anything left for you to rule."

Before she could respond, the Ace of Clubs stepped in on her behalf. "I won't have you talking to the Queen like that." He started toward Douglas. "This ends now!" The Ace lifted his spear, ready to strike when—

Douglas leveled his weapon and sent a bullet through the Ace's chest.

Stunned, the soldier stumbled, his expression locked in a mix of terror and disbelief. Out of control, he fell forward, his body coming to an abrupt halt when he inadvertently impaled himself on his own spear.

"Anyone else want to die for her Majesty?" Douglas asked.

Horrified, the Queen looked down at the Ace. His body was propped up by the spear so he appeared frozen in free-fall. Strangely, there was no blood where the bullet had entered the Ace's chest, just a singed, dime-sized puncture that was enough to see the playing-card men really were made of paper.

Douglas softened his tone as he continued. "It didn't have to be this way, your Highness, but now it does. How your story ends is completely up to you."

Trembling, the Queen lowered her gaze then bowed her head.

"Tell them," Douglas said.

She swallowed hard. "He is the new Ace."

Nothing more than a wavered breath, the words barely escaped her lips.

"So they can hear you."

"He is the new Ace!"

"And the kids?"

"The children aren't to be harmed!"

Douglas turned to face the soldiers grouped nearby. He gave them a moment to act, but none was willing to step forward like the Ace.

"We're going after the children," Douglas said. "Be ready to leave right away."

With that, Douglas gestured for Hope to join him on his way into the castle.

When they were gone, the lawn came alive with whispers and murmurs. The jabbering filled the Queen with rage, her emotions quickly heating to a rolling boil. Hook watched as she looked about, swinging her attention from one part of the crowd to the next. Everyone averted their eyes just as they normally would... but they didn't stop talking. Not this time. The people of Wonderland weren't nearly as scared of the Queen as they'd been before her altercation with Douglas.

"Boy," Smee began, "that was something. Did you see what he did?"

Lost in thought, Hook didn't respond. There was no cold glare to shut Smee up; no smack across the back of the head to remind him of his place.

"What's wrong, capt'n? Didn't you see? Stanford's going to give us weapons like that when we're through. This war with Pan is all but over. You've finally won."

Hook patted his companion on the back. "Maybe you're right, Smee."

A broad smile lit Smee's face. "Did you hear that, boys? The captain says I might be right." The tubby pirate skipped over to the join the rest of Hook's crew.

"Hey e'rybody! Smee was finally right about something."

Hook's men laughed, a few congratulating Smee on a job well done.

Hook had an urge to remind them that even his broken clocks were right twice a day, but he decided against it.

He had more pressing things to think about.

CHAPTER 12

RANDY AND TAY walked the woods in silence. Randy tried getting Taylor to talk, but all she offered in response were grunts and nods. Finally, after more than an hour, Randy fell back on old habits...

"A thank you would be nice," he said snidely.

"You have *got* to be kidding me."

"I saved your life back there."

"And I save yours. We're even."

"You can't even bring yourself to fake it, can you?"

"Did you ever think I had a plan? That I didn't need your help to begin with?"

"Your plan was about to get your head chopped off. I guess I should have let that happen, huh? I mean: you'd be dead, but as least you wouldn't have to be nice to me."

"So what are we supposed to do now? Were you smart enough to grab your dad's amulet? Because without it we have no way of getting home."

Tay stormed down the path so Randy was left behind. Like always, she'd made sure to get the last word. Randy hated that. There was nothing worse than being put in your place by one of those front-of-the-class kids who always had the answers. And yet, right now, he didn't feel like he'd been bested by one of the school's biggest know-it-alls...

He felt like he'd let down a friend.

"I didn't think about that," he said softly. "I just... I was scared, okay? I really thought they were gonna kill you. And my dad... he just stood there. I didn't mean to get us stuck in the woods, but I wasn't thinking that far ahead."

The sincerity in Randy's voice was enough to make Taylor think twice about her tone. She tried to catch his eye, but he wouldn't let her. After trying to get her to open up for most of the afternoon, Randy was finally done.

They continued down the path in silence. It was nearly dusk when the road diverged in opposite directions.

Randy gestured to the choice ahead of them. "Which way, genius?"

Taylor looked down each of the paths before them. Darkness was coming so quickly that she couldn't see much. She turned to find Randy waiting impatiently, his expression like anger chiseled in stone.

"I don't know..."

Randy shook his head like he wasn't surprised.

Neither spoke for a long moment, the tension thick between them.

"I didn't have a plan either," Taylor finally said.

Her confession softened him a bit.

"I was going to make a run for it when they got me to the end of the field, but I wasn't worried about the amulet – I just wanted to get away."

"If you didn't have a plan, why'd you say that you did?"

Taylor shrugged the question away, and Randy didn't press. They were finally talking. He didn't want to risk burning the bridge they were finally beginning to mend.

CHAPTER 13

WESLEY AND THE Librarian quickly discovered they had more work to do upon returning to Astoria's library. After waiting for the portal to close behind them, both hurried into the building's main hall only to come to an abrupt halt when they saw what had become of the library.

"Holy cow!" Wesley exclaimed. "What happened?"

A web of cracks had formed in the building's ceiling. Several of the fissures were large enough that jagged pieces of stone had broken free. Even worse, the room's domed skylight had shattered, collapsing to the floor and dusting it with shards of centuries-old glass.

"Did we do this?"

The old man shook his head. "I don't believe so," he said. "It seems Douglas has done even more damage since leaving Oz."

Glass crunched beneath his sneakers as Wesley wandered through the wreckage. All of the literature displays had toppled over and created a jumbled mess on the floor. *Pan* relics were piled alongside items that had fallen from the *Oz* display. Riches from *Treasure Island* were hidden beneath Tom Sawyer's hat.

As Wes tried to make sense of it all, The Librarian crossed the room to a window near the building's lobby. After looking outside, the old man sighed.

"What is it?" Wesley asked. "What's wrong?"

The Librarian turned. Wes thought the lines in his face looked deeper now.

"It's nothing you want to see," the old man explained.

But that wasn't true. Wesley was already hurrying over to see what had left his companion so distraught. He needed the boost of a nearby chair to get a good look but nearly fell to the floor when he saw what was waiting outside.

While the library's parking lot was untouched, everything beyond the gate was blanketed in ash. Across the street, the windows on storefronts were boarded up, their walls wrapped in overgrowth. Burned-out cars sat abandoned in the street, and no one was walking the brick sidewalks today.

But it wasn't the absence of life that unsettled Wes. An unnatural haze was draped across the sky just above the city's skyline. It was just enough to prevent the sun's warmth from reaching the surface, as if there to ensure life would never return to Astoria again.

Evil had taken over in Oz after their trip into the storybook land, but this was different. Evil did not exist in this world. Neither did good. This was what the world looked like after a war with no winners finally comes to its end.

Wesley hopped down from the chair. "It looks like a bomb went off!"

The old man nodded. "As I said: I believe Douglas has been busy."

"What could have caused something like this?"

The Librarian pointed to the window. "This is our reality without any of your favorite books."

"You're saying Randy's dad has rewritten every story in two days?"

"Of course not. But you know better than anyone, small changes to the course of history can have a dramatic effect. A ripple here, a ripple there..."

Wesley stood with his mouth agape. It had been hard enough to set things right in Oz, and he still wasn't certain they had accomplished that. How were they going to fix this? Could they? Was it even possible? If they couldn't, did that mean they would have to spend the rest of their days living in a wasteland?

The old man seemed to read Wesley's mind. "Let's focus our attention on what we can control. Your priority has always been to find Miss Taylor. If we put our focus there, I imagine we'll come across Douglas along the way."

Wes shrugged. "How are we supposed to find them?"

The Librarian started down one of the aisles. "We read."

CHAPTER 14

AFTER WATCHING DOUGLAS lead a group of her soldiers into the forest, the Queen of Hearts had retreated to her chambers alone. She'd stationed two sentries outside the door, but that had not been enough to sooth her nerves. She'd burst into tears as soon as the door was closed behind her. It had taken everything she had to keep from doing it in front of her subjects. Even now that the tears were subsiding, she couldn't keep her hands from shaking.

Her tears were nearly dried when someone knocked on her door. The Queen quickly steeled herself with a series of deep breaths before answering. "Come!"

A guard pushed his head through the doorway.

"I thought I made it clear I wasn't to be disturbed."

"It's one of the outsiders, your Majesty."

Suddenly nervous, the Queen swallowed hard.

"Did... did something happen to his son?"

The guard leaned forward so he could talk in a lower voice and still be heard. "It's the other gentleman. The one who's missing a hand."

The Queen wasn't sure what to make of this, but she motioned for the guard to allow Hook into her chambers. While waiting, she fixed her posture and straightened the crown on her head. When Hook entered, the Queen looked to be her normal, intimidating self.

The pirate immediately fell to one knee upon entering.

"I see someone from the outside world knows how to treat royalty."

"I do, indeed. But you shouldn't think of me as an outsider."

"Why's that? Pray tell."

Hook got to his feet. "Because we're both living in the same prison."

The Queen scoffed. "This looks like a prison to you?"

"How else would you describe it?"

"I rule all of Wonderland. I'm free to do as I please. People are forced to do what I say or they lose their heads. I don't know what to call it, but I'd say it's the opposite of a prison – wouldn't you?"

"That's how it's meant to appear, your Highness. That way you don't question things. But if you believe what Stanford has said... there's no other word for it."

Hook saw the Queen didn't understand.

"Give this some thought," he explained. "You're trapped in a loop, living out the same days over-and-over again. All of your circumstances are controlled by those books the girl described – what does that sound like? Do you really think you're in control if you have to be embarrassed by Alice again and again and again... for all eternity?"

The Queen's mouth twisted into a frown. "Do you believe him?"

"I can tell you that he lied about being a king," Hook said. "That was just something to curry your favor. But I do know what he says about these magic books is true. Even worse: I think the girl was being honest, too."

"So why are you helping him?" the Queen asked.

"He promised me weapons to defeat the children who torment me in Neverland."

The Queen chuckled. "It all comes back to that. These awful children."

"I don't know that I blame them. Their actions are controlled by words on a page the same as ours. In a way, you and Alice have suffered the same fate."

The Queen wanted to refute this, but there was nothing she could say.

"At least Stanford has offered us a chance to change the story."

"Perhaps," Hook said. "But we'll still be living out the same days over-and-over again."

"I'm not sure we have another option."

"Yes we do," Hook explained. "The real world."

"Stanford's land?"

"His people live a life the way it's meant to be lived. Why stay in these prisons they've created for us when the freedom of choice is just a portal away?"

"But... I wouldn't be Queen."

Hook nodded like he knew this response was coming. "I've considered that, your Highness. Stanford wants our help to retrieve the most powerful book from his world – one that will allow him to control events in this real world the way these authors have controlled the events in ours."

The corner of the Queen's mouth lifted into a black grin. "We could get the book for ourselves. Then we would hold the pen."

"Exactly," Hook said. "Why live like royalty... if we can be gods?"

CHAPTER 15

JUST AFTER SUNSET, Douglas and the Queen's soldiers happened upon the dead playing-card men in the clearing. The soldiers were horrified to see what was left of their compatriots. Their faces were bruised and bloody, but their paper bodies had been burned to a crisp. The ashes that remained were already starting to blow away in the wind.

The Nine looked to the King beside him. "Those children didn't do this."

"You don't think..."

"What else could it have been?"

Douglas listened to them go on about the Jabberwock. He didn't add anything but suspected they might be wrong about who (or what) had brought death down on the two soldiers.

Several of the playing-card men were studying tracks in the dirt nearby.

"Is there any real sign the Jabberwock was here?" Douglas asked.

"No sir," the Six explained. "There was a struggle, but we would know if the Jabberwock was involved. Its tracks are unmistakable."

"What about the children?"

"It looks like they were cornered in this tree."

"See if you can pick up a trail that leads out of this clearing," Douglas ordered.

"Yes, sir."

The Six led his companion to the clearing's edge where they began searching for clues. When they were gone, Douglas turned to inspect the mammoth tree in the center of the clearing. A spear was jutting out from the tree's trunk, still there from the attack on Randy and Tay. Douglas could only imagine how scared the kids must have been in that moment. And yet, that wasn't what concerned him most. Douglas hated that Randy thought this was something he had to do in the first place. Whether he liked the girl or not, Douglas knew he should have been the one to step in to help her – not his boy.

❖ ❖ ❖

While neither was ready to admit it, Randy and Taylor were both getting scared now that the sun had gone down. The woods were impossibly dark. They could barely see each other, let alone the path they were walking. Not only that, a strange hush had fallen over the forest. Randy had worried the night would come alive with activity, but the opposite had happened. Somehow, that was worse. The quiet was deafening and seemed to pressurize the air around them.

"How long are we just going to walk in the dark like this?" Randy asked.

"The farther we get from that castle, the better."

They continued forward, neither talking until Taylor noticed a flicker of light filtering through the trees from somewhere nearby.

"Look," she said. "Someone's there."

"That's a good thing?" Randy asked.

"Maybe they can help."

"Tay, no one will be able to help us get home."

"Right now I'm just hoping we can get something to eat."

Randy had to agree with that. His stomach felt like it was going to collapse on itself at any moment.

Together the kids stepped from the path toward the light in the distance. It was difficult to navigate this dense part of the forest in the dark, but it wasn't long before the two came to a stone wall bordering the property of a small cottage. Passing through its gate, the kids saw candles inside the cabin were the source of the light that had pulled them from the trail.

Tay eased up the steps onto the patio then knocked on the cabin's front door.

No one answered.

"Hello? We're sorry to bother you this late, but we could really use your help."

Randy peered through one of the windows. "No one's home."

"You're sure?"

"Positive."

"Do you think we should wait?" Taylor asked.

Randy brushed past her. "You're the one who wanted to race over here." He pushed the door open and stepped inside the cottage. "No sense stopping a few feet short of the finish line."

This time it was Tay who lagged behind. "Randy? That's someone's house!"

When Randy didn't answer, Taylor hurried into the cabin behind him.

Neither noticed someone watching from the darkness nearby. In fact, by the time the hidden soldier had motioned for his playing-card friends to join him, Taylor had already shut the door behind them.

◆ ◆ ◆

Douglas awkwardly climbed the rocky hillside. Above the tree line, several playing-card soldiers were scattered all around him in search of a trail. They'd done a remarkable job tracking the kids so far, but the tracks had become harder to follow in the darkness. The rocky terrain only made things worse.

As they searched for clues, Douglas started toward a trickling waterfall just ahead of him. It glimmered in the moonlight, the water reflecting the night sky so it looked like a string of diamonds spilling down the mountain's face.

Douglas dipped a hand into the water for a drink. He'd taken several sips from his cupped hands when his attention fell on something nearby.

He knelt down, eyes fixed on the smashed pumpkin at his feet. Turning one of the broken pieces over, Douglas saw half of the Jack-O-Lantern's cutout face.

"Bones..."

Douglas felt his throat tighten.

Despite years of planning, decades even, his plans were starting to fall apart. And now his son was wrapped up in this nonsense, too. The library's magic had already taken so much from him. Was it about to take something more?

Just then there was a rustle of movement in the brush nearby.

Douglas shot to his feet.

The soldiers quickly turned toward the tree line, weapons ready when—

A member of the pack came sprinting out of the forest.

Everyone sighed in relief as the playing-card man hurried over to join them.

"What is it?" the Six asked. "What's wrong?"

Short on breath, it took the new face a moment to respond. "It's the children," he said between gasps. "We've found them."

CHAPTER 16

THE QUEEN HAD promised Hook she would enlist her best men to help in their quest, but Hook was beginning to wonder if he was walking into a double-cross. She'd led him into the bowels of her castle. They had traded tile floor for dirt. Walls of polished marble had been replaced by chiseled stone that leaked water. The place reeked of decay.

"Where are we going?" Hook asked. "This looks like the dungeon."

The Queen shook her head. "My prisoners are kept in the east wing. That way I'm not bothered with their screams. This is where my babies stay."

She started down a long corridor toward a single door. The door certainly looked like the entrance to a cell: the kind where prisoners are left and forgotten.

The pirate's hand found the hilt of his sword as they continued forward.

"There's a reason I need the entire pack of cards to do my bidding," the Queen said. "They're a collection of bumbling fools. It takes that many to do the work of a single squad of men. Unless we're talking about my Jokers."

When they reached the cell door, he watched as the Queen looked into the darkness beyond the barred window. It was the first time since meeting her that Hook saw something soft in the woman's eyes – almost loving.

"Are you rested, my beauties?"

She pressed her fat cheek to the door and began rubbing its surface with her palm as if that would sooth whoever was locked away inside.

"Children have returned to Wonderland. It's time to sharpen your blades."

❖ ❖ ❖

"Is anyone home?" Taylor asked.

Lit by candlelight, there was nothing unusual about the cottage. It was a single-room cabin with a cozy sitting-area arranged near a stone fireplace. A table stood near the fire with a chess set should anyone be interested enough to play. A single bed was pressed against the opposite wall. Bookshelves took up one corner of the room while another was dedicated to the kitchen. It was in the kitchen that something unusual finally caught Taylor's eye.

"Come here," she said. "Look."

"What is it?" Randy asked.

Plated on the kitchen table, a single piece of cake with pastel frosting waited for anyone who entered the cottage. A note had been left beside the dessert, two words scrawled across the thick piece of parchment in near-perfect calligraphy.

"Eat me," Randy read aloud. "Hey! Don't mind if I do."

Randy reached for the cake, but Tay grabbed his hand before he could get it.

"You're the one who said we need to eat," Randy reminded.

"Not that."

"Why not?"

"You don't remember?" Taylor asked. "In the book Alice eats a piece of cake after reading a note like that – she ends up growing to be like fifty feet tall."

Frustrated, Randy shook his head. This was starting to get ridiculous.

"This girl seems to know a bit more than the last. Don't you think?"

Startled, Taylor spun toward the sound of this new voice.

"Who is that? Who's there?"

"Umm... Taylor? Look."

Randy stood in the center of the room, brow scrunched, his attention fixed on the sitting-area near the fireplace. Tay followed his gaze until it landed on the chess set. Curiously, the chess pieces were not arranged in their normal positions when set for a game. Stepping forward, Taylor realized some of the pieces weren't on the board at all.

But that wasn't what made the chess set so peculiar.

On closer inspection, Taylor saw...

The chess pieces were alive!

Blinking eyes stared up at the children; chests moved in-and-out as the pieces breathed. The tiny figures moved as if the gods had breathed life into their wooden bodies. Tay tried to blink the vision away, but she couldn't, not even when the Black Queen stepped forward and took a bow.

"Hello," she began, "My name is Queen Jezebel. Welcome to my kingdom."

Before Taylor could respond, another of the pieces cleared her throat.

"Excuse me?" The Queen carved from lighter woods stepped forward, clearly taking exception to what Jezebel had said. "If I remember correctly, we won the last game. That would make the board *my* kingdom."

"That game didn't count, Adrienne. We were guided by children."

"I don't see why that should matter."

"Because they were six years old! Neither knew how to play when they sat down – they were just moving us around the board like toys."

Adrienne stuck her chin into the air and crossed her arms. "It doesn't matter. A game is a game, and that's a game the white team won."

Jezebel snorted disapproval. "One of the *only* games you've won."

"What was that?" Adrienne asked, her voice sharp enough to cut.

"Nothing..."

A number of pieces voiced their disapproval in a chorus of groans. Some looked away, rolling their eyes as if this argument had been going on for years. When the protests began to subside, one of the white knights rode his wooden horse to the front of the group.

"Young lady," he said in a gruff voice. "I wonder if you'll inform me of your companion's intentions?"

"I'm sorry?" Taylor responded.

"I'm not comfortable with the way the boy is staring at us," the knight explained. "If he means to do battle, I'd appreciate he do us the courtesy of announcing his intentions now."

"What? No." Taylor looked over to find Randy had yet to pick his jaw off the floor. "He doesn't want to battle. Do you, Randy?"

He didn't answer until Tay jabbed him with her elbow.

"No... no, I don't want to... to battle."

Jezebel scooted to the edge of the table. "Then why are you children here?"

"Well," Taylor began, "it's hard to explain. We're looking for help. We're trapped in Wonderland and need to get back to our world."

"Then you may have happened upon the right place," Adrienne said.

"Why do you say that?"

"People have used the mirror to visit Wonderland. I suppose one could pass through it in the opposite direction."

Adrienne gestured to an ornate mirror on the wall over the fireplace. When she saw it, a broad smile lit Taylor's face. "You have to be kidding me."

"I don't get it," Randy said. "What's so funny?"

"It's the Looking Glass: the mirror Alice uses to

come into Wonderland."

♦ ♦ ♦

As the children were becoming acquainted with their new friends in the cottage, half-a-dozen playing-card men were circling the cabin outside. No need to hide their presence at this point, the soldiers lit torches to help them see in the darkness as they planned their next move.

"Should we go inside after them?" the Jack asked his King.

"Not yet. We'll wait for the outsider to give his go-ahead. Just make sure we've covered the exits in case they try to escape."

The Jack responded with a nod then led a few of the numbered cards around the corner toward the rear of the cabin. When they were gone, the King was left alone with the Ten near the property's border wall.

"There's a skylight," the Ten explained. "I could get a look at what's happening inside without being seen."

The King looked into the forest like he was hoping Douglas would appear so he wouldn't have to give the order. When no one came, he nodded an affirmation and the Ten hurried off to climb onto the cabin's roof.

♦ ♦ ♦

Taylor stepped forward to study the mirror over the fireplace.

"I thought Alice fell down a rabbit hole," Randy said.

"The first time. When she comes back: it's through this mirror."

Taylor put her hand flush against the mirror's face. When she did, the glass rippled like water as her hand pushed through to the other side.

"Whoa!" Randy exclaimed.

Giggling a bit, Tay wiggled her fingers on the other side of the mirror.

So that's it, right? Our ticket home?"

At this, Taylor's face finally fell. "Not really," she said.

"What do you mean?"

"The mirror won't take us back to the library."

"Right now we're just trying to get out of Wonderland."

"But do you really want to end up in England? England in the 1900s?"

The ripples had dissipated so the glass was smooth, but Taylor had kept her arm in place. The idea that Taylor's hand was somehow trapped in the past left Randy with a feeling of apprehension. He was relieved when she finally pulled her hand back into their world.

"Truthfully," Taylor began, "I don't even know if that's the real England."

"What do you mean?"

Tay saw the chess pieces were listening to their

conversation. She leaned in for a private word with Randy. "Alice lives in the book just like they do, right? That means she has to live somewhere in the storybook lands. She may live in England, but it's not the England in our world. It's... different."

"A fake version of the real thing," Randy muttered.

Taylor nodded.

"So we're still stuck? There's nothing else we can do?"

"I'm doing the best I can here!"

Randy winced at her biting tone. This time, Taylor noticed.

"I'm sorry," she said. "I didn't mean for it to come out that way."

"No... it's okay."

"No it's not. I wouldn't have gotten away without your help."

This seemed to boost Randy's spirits. "Yeah?"

Taylor nodded. Blushing a bit, Randy smiled back at her. They held each other's gaze for a long moment, neither sure what to say until—

The skylight overhead shattered!

Both looked up to find a playing-card soldier crashing down on them in a shower of broken glass.

The kids ducked for cover as the soldier landed flat on his back. Randy locked eyes with the intruder. Then both shifted their attention to the soldier's spear. The weapon had fallen to the floor so it sat equal distance between them. When he saw it, Randy lunged forward, sliding on his belly through the bed of broken glass. His fingers grazed the spear's wrapped handle, ready to grab hold when the soldier threw himself down on Randy.

Pinned beneath his attacker, Randy struggled to break free. It was like fighting a heavy blanket that thwarted his every effort to escape. Eventually, the playing-card man got the best of him. With the spear in hand, the soldier stood up and pinned Randy beneath one of his feet. "In the name of her Highness, the Queen of Hearts, I hereby place you under arrest."

Apparently forgotten, Taylor leapt from the shadows. She threw her shoulder into the soldier so he was forced to shift his weight in an effort to keep his balance...

It was all the break Randy needed.

Randy stumbled to his feet as the soldier regained his footing. The warrior thrust his spear in a savage strike. Randy leapt back on his heels just in time to see the spear plunge past him.

"Taylor! Get out of here!"

Snarling, the soldier spun around to face the boy. Randy made a move at him, but the intruder jabbed him in the stomach with the blunt end of his spear. Randy doubled over in pain.

With Randy down, the playing-card man turned his gaze to Taylor. She froze. The soldier twirled his spear until its arrowhead tip was in the lead so he could impale the young girl once within striking distance.

Taylor backed into the kitchen.

Closing in, the soldier tossed the kitchen table aside with a single hand.

Watching from the chessboard, the pieces were beginning to panic.

"We have to do something!" Jezebel exclaimed.

"What can we do?" Adrienne asked.

"Just give the order," a knight said. "We'll do what we can."

Adrienne was about to do just that when she saw Randy had finally recovered. "Look!"

Seeing the soldier had backed Taylor into the corner, Randy darted across the room and pulled the mirror from the wall.

"What is he doing?" Jezebel wondered aloud.

Tay felt her backside brush the kitchen counter. She had nowhere left to go.

"Don't worry," the soldier sneered. "This shouldn't hurt too much."

Taylor's body tensed up. But her fear quickly gave way to confusion when she saw Randy lugging the mirror toward them.

"Hey! Thin man!"

The soldier turned, stunned to learn the boy was back on his feet. Wasting no time, Randy lifted the awkward mirror into the air then let gravity do the rest. He guided the mirror so it landed flush against the soldier's head. Strangely, the impact didn't slow the mirror down or change its path. Instead, the soldier's head pushed through the mirror's face just as Taylor's hand had a few moments before. Gaining speed, the mirror swallowed the attacker whole on its way to the floor. When the Looking Glass finally landed near Randy's feet, the playing-card man had disappeared beneath it – trapped in another world.

◆ ◆ ◆

Douglas stepped into the clearing. Anger reddened his cheeks when he saw all of the Clubs had surrounded the tiny cottage with their torches. His furious gaze landed on the broken skylight in the cabin's roof.

"What was that noise?" Douglas demanded. "What did you do?"

The King of Clubs stammered. "The Ten... he... well..."

"I thought I told you to wait."

"I saw no reason we shouldn't confirm the children were inside. And... well... now that we've lost the element of surprise, we're prepared to fire the cottage on your command."

Douglas glared at the squad leader. "That's my son!"

"I understand. But if we're to apprehend the children–"

"No one is to do another thing until I give the order. Is that understood?" Douglas yelled the order loud enough that even those behind the house knew they were to keep hold of their torches. He looked to the King to repeat his order.

"Stand ready, men. Hold your ground."

Douglas started toward the front door.

"You don't think you can get them to come out willingly?" the King asked.

"He's my son," Douglas explained. "He'll do what I tell him."

❖ ❖ ❖

Randy rushed to the window for a look outside.

"Well," Jezebel began, smoothing her dress, "that was exciting!"

Taylor joined Randy. "What's going on?" she asked.

"See for yourself."

Taylor joined Randy and saw Douglas was marching toward the front door.

"Any ideas?" Randy asked.

Taylor looked about the room. "I'm working on it."

"We could make a run for it."

"That didn't work last time."

"We don't have any other options."

Taylor's attention fell to the kitchen floor.

"We'll fight them off," she murmured.

"Uhh... how are we gonna do that?"

Taylor hurried into the kitchen and foraged through the wreckage left behind from their fight with the soldier. She rose to her feet with the piece of white cake in hand, a smushed mess.

"We'll eat the cake. We'll fight them when we're big."

"What about the five-second rule?" Randy joked.

Tay ignored him. "Besides, running away will be easier when we're ten times our normal size."

"Then what? We're fifty-feet tall the rest of our lives."

"If Alice went back to normal, so can we."

"There's an easier way," a familiar voice explained.

Both kids wheeled around to find Randy's dad standing in the doorway.

"You won't have to run at all if you just come with me."

❖ ❖ ❖

Outside the squad of playing-card soldiers remained circled around the cottage with their torches in hand. While most were hoping to get a sense of what was happening inside, many were flashing sideways glances toward the King to see if he would give a second order. Eventually, the Jack joined him near the tree line so he could share what the others were thinking.

"This is madness," he whispered.

"I don't like it any more than you do. But you saw what he did to the Ace."

"So now we're trapped between this outsider and the Queen?"

"I'm not sure which one is worse."

The Jack was about to respond when there was movement in the darkness behind them. It wasn't much: limbs bending and leaves shuffling as something made its way through the woods towards them.

"What's that?" the Jack asked nervously.

"I'm not sure..."

But the King's fear suggested otherwise. The movement had been accompanied by an unnatural sound that had no business in the woods. It was eerie, enough to make the hair on your neck prickle: a rattle-and-click that sounded like rocks grinding against one another... or bones.

Click-clack, click-clack.

The soldiers watched in terror as the shadows came alive.

Clickety-clack, clickety-clack.

Dark shapes swooshed around in the black.

Louder now, closer, right on top of them—

Something leapt out from the trees. Nothing but a blur, the dark shadow snatched one of the soldiers and pulled him into the forest.

Another followed. This time, two white arms extended from the blackness to grab the second soldier before disappearing into the night with its captive.

"What was that?!" the Jack shouted. *"What's happening?"*

The soldiers helplessly listened as their companions were dragged away.

Trembling, those that remained tightened their grips on their torches, ready to swing them at anything that might leap from the shadows again.

Each scanned the darkness, eyes searching for any sign of the dark attackers. But all they saw were the dual flames of the stolen torches as someone picked them up from the ground and started toward them once more.

"They're coming," the Jack said nervously. "What are we supposed to do?"

"We'll thank the stars that they aren't here for us," the King explained.

◆ ◆ ◆

Douglas stepped toward his son. "Don't just stand there."

Randy backed away. "I'm not going with you!"

"You don't understand. The Queen's has promised to forgive you both."

Taylor gestured to the mirror on the floor. "One of her creepy playing-card soldiers just tried to kill us!"

"That was before," Douglas explained. "They know I'm in charge."

"Oh!" Taylor exclaimed. "I fell so much better."

Growing frustrated, Douglas shifted his attention to Randy. "We have to go."

"I know. You have to hurry back so you can finish building your army."

"Randal, I know you're confused, but..."

"I'm confused? What do you think is gonna happen when you start rewriting your childhood? What if *I* end up in an orphanage just like you did?"

Douglas inched forward. "That won't happen. We'll have the power to change anything we want. The past, the present, the future. We'll control it all."

"Wow! That doesn't sound evil at all, dad."

Douglas looked over at Tay, embarrassed to know she was there to witness the back-and-forth with his son. He checked the cuffs on his shirt then smoothed the front of his jacket. "What do you think I'm after, son? You think I want the library's magic so I can use it to get rich and empower myself?"

"Honestly? I think you want revenge."

Douglas opened his mouth to defend himself, but the words caught in his throat. For a moment, he looked totally exposed, as if his son had shined a light on his darkest thoughts, thoughts he'd hidden so well he didn't even know they were there. "W-what's wrong with that?" he asked.

"Nothing," Randy said. "If you're a pirate."

Taylor stood beside Randy, unsure how his father would respond to the accusation. Even the chess pieces were quiet, each of them perched near the end of the table until—

"Watch out!"

The children flinched as a torch came crashing through a nearby window. When it touched the ground its fire danced across the floor and ignited the curtains.

"I knew it!" Taylor screamed. *"He's here to distract us!"*

Ignoring the accusation, Douglas turned toward

the front door. *"No! What are you doing?"*

A second torch crashed through a window at the back of the room.

"Here!" Taylor exclaimed. "Quick!"

Tay split the cake in two and handed a fistful of the dessert to Randy. Both shoveled a handful into their mouth.

Douglas charged forward, reaching out for his son. *"No! Don't!"*

But it was too late. The children were already beginning to change.

Only neither grew the way they had hoped.

The cake worked its magic on them one bit at a time. Taylor's head shriveled up until it was no larger than a grape sitting atop her shoulders. Her legs came next, thinning out until they looked like limp noodles unable to support her weight.

For Randy, the metamorphosis happened in reverse. His arms lost their length, thinning and telescoping into his body until his hands looked like they were dangling from tiny threads tied to his shoulders. Looking down at himself was almost enough to make Randy sick. Luckily, the rest of him quickly followed suit, everything withering away until he was just an inch tall, shorter even than their new friends on the chessboard.

Towering over them, Douglas leaned forward like he was going to scoop both children up from the floor. *"It's okay! Stay there! Don't move!"*

Randy and Tay darted into the kitchen so they could hide among the mess.

"Randal!"

His voice was as loud as thunder. Both kids covered their ears as they ducked beneath the folds of the fallen tablecloth.

Douglas tore through the clutter to find them. *"Please! Don't do this!"*

The kids pulled together behind some spilled dishes in the corner.

Nothing but a firestorm now, the cottage crumbled all around them. Curtains that framed each of the home's tiny windows were ablaze. The books on a nearby shelf spewed glowing cinders into the air as they burned. An orange and blue wave of flames seemed to defy gravity as it spread across the ceiling's surface, rafters shifting in the wave's wake as the fire ate away at them.

"Randy! Let me help you!"

A rafter dislodged from the ceiling and crashed to the floor. Leaping for cover, Douglas narrowly escaped. He rose to his feet, took one final look around the room, then backed his way toward the exit and disappeared through the door.

Watching from the kitchen, Randy couldn't believe it. "He... he left."

"Only because he thinks we're already gone."

Inching into the open, Taylor shielded her face from the fire's heat. Nearby, the chess pieces were helping each other down to the floor.

"How exactly are we gonna get out of here?" Randy said.

Tay ignored the question, pointing to something

in the distance. "Look!"

A mouse was scurrying across the floor. On all fours, it instinctively dodged falling debris as it hurried toward Randy and Tay. The mouse fell onto its hind legs when it was close enough to join them. Both kids smiled when they saw it was wearing a plaid vest and sporting wire spectacles on the end of its nose.

"I suppose the two of you could use some help," Father Mouse said.

"Do you know a way out of here?" Taylor asked.

"Of course! We'll use the front door."

With that, Father Mouse took off. The kids sprinted behind him, but they struggled to keep pace. Randy would later recall he felt like his face was going to melt off. Fiery debris was now crashing to the floor at an alarming rate. At their new diminutive size, even one of the scorching embers floating down from the bookshelf would be enough to incinerate their bodies on contact.

"This is stupid!" Randy shouted. *"We're never gonna make it!"*

But then Randy's gaze fell on the crack beneath the door. There was just enough room for him and Taylor to shimmy beneath the door and escape.

If they made it—

All at once, an umbrella stand near the door toppled into their path. It left a fan of flame hanging in its wake.

The three of them slid to a stop, cowering as the stand crashed to the floor in front of them – a fiery barricade between them and the cottage door.

There was no getting around it and no climbing over.

Their only path to escape was now blocked.

"Now what?" Taylor screamed over the fire.

The Mouse looked about the room. *"The passage! Hurry!"*

"What?" Randy shouted. "What passage?"

Father Mouse rose up on his hind legs and pointed into the kitchen. All of the chess pieces were filing into a cabinet beneath the sink.

"That'll get us out of here?" Taylor asked.

"It's the only way."

The mouse took off again, weaving in-and-out of the fallen debris and rising flames. Unfortunately, Randy and Tay weren't able to move as fast. The air's temperature had risen to an unbearable degree. Black smoke now filled most of the room. Coughing violently, the kids started after the mouse but quickly fell behind. Neither looked like they would make it.

From the kitchen, one of the black knights gestured to the struggling kids. *"Knights!"*

Showing no signs of fear, all four of the mounted knights charged straight into the fire. Every time something blocked their path – a piece of debris, a pocket of fire – they changed course, picking up speed the entire way until they reached the kids. Once there, two of the knights scooped the kids up and threw them onto their horses.

"We'll take it from here," one of them said.

The ride back was more of a challenge. Their escape nearly came to an abrupt end when the knights discovered the kitchen table and discarded tablecloth were now ablaze like everything else.

"Hold tight, my lady."

Seeing her knight wasn't going to slow down, Tay did as he said, wrapping both arms around the horse as they picked up speed. When they reached the wall of flame, the horses leapt through the fire, all four landing unscathed near the cabinet where several of the chess pieces stood waiting with Father Mouse.

"Well!" the mouse exclaimed. "It doesn't get much closer than that!"

Taylor's knight lowered her from the horse to the floor. Randy's did the same.

"Thank you," Taylor said.

The knights bowed their heads in response.

"Now," Father Mouse began, "Quickly! In here!"

The mouse climbed into the kitchen cabinet, making sure the others followed before disappearing into the darkness. Once inside, Randy and Tay got to their feet and took in their new surroundings. They stood on a wooden shelf where several pots and pans were neatly stacked. Somehow, standing inside the cabinet had dulled the deafening fire in the cottage to a quiet roar.

"Follow him," one of the knights instructed. "To the back."

"Where are we going?" Randy asked.

Already heading that way, the knight didn't

answer. It wasn't until Randy and Tay rounded the giant pots and pans that they understood why...

A mouse hole near the back of the cabinet opened up into the wall.

"This will take us out?" Taylor asked nervously.

"It should," Father Mouse explained. "Only... it may get a little hot."

He gestured for the kids to step into the passage. When they did, Randy saw their escape wasn't going to get any easier. The passage was nothing more than a narrow corridor filled with smoke and wallpapered in orange flame. And yet, he saw there was light at the end of the tunnel. Escape was only a few feet away. There was actually a chance they would make it out...

If they didn't burn to death first.

CHAPTER 17

THE COTTAGE LIT up the night, spitting embers that flittered through the air like fireflies as Douglas stumbled out of the fiery building.

Hacking smoke, he started toward the King of Clubs, screaming at the soldier before he'd covered the distance between them. *"What did I say? I think I know what I said because I was standing there when I said it!"*

"You don't understand!" the King explained. *"It wasn't my fault!"*

"The Ace is dead! If I didn't give the order—"

"My men didn't throw those torches!"

Douglas looked about. A few of the soldiers were eavesdropping, but most had fixed their eyes on the forest around them. They no longer held their torches as a source of light. Each was gripping his torch in trembling hands, ready to swing it at anything that might appear from within the web of shadows.

"Do you think I'm an idiot?" Douglas asked. "There's no one else here."

When the King didn't respond, the Eight stepped forward.

"It was the Jokers," he explained.

"What?"

"Every pack has two Jokers. And now the Queen's are after your son."

Douglas looked about once more. "If that's true – where are they?"

"They've slipped into the dark," the King said. "They always do."

"They're hiding?"

The Eight shook his head. "The Jokers don't hide from anyone."

"What happened to your son?" the King asked.

"He... he's eaten the cake... he's small now." Douglas held his finger and thumb a few inches apart to show just what he meant.

"That may be the only thing that saves his life."

Douglas looked toward the cabin. The flames reached as high as the trees around them. It looked as if the blaze could reach out and grab any one of them, something that would mean certain death for the cardboard men. And yet, the soldiers were more focused on the shadows around them.

They feared the Jokers more than they feared the flame.

"They couldn't have gotten far," Douglas began, "not at their size. We'll spread out, begin our search along the east side of the house. That's where I saw them last. Tell your men to be careful where they step. I don't want anyone to inadvertently step on either of the kids."

"I can't do that, sir."

"You can and you will."

Without a word, the King lifted his chin in

defiance.

"Do I have to remind you *why* you're taking orders from me? Assemble your men."

The King laid his spear at Douglas's feet. Enraged, Douglas pulled his pistol and leveled it at the King's cardboard chest. But the King did not move.

"I was there to watch as you killed the Ace, but I'd rather die as he did than face the Jokers. I think you'll find my men feel the same."

Douglas passed his gaze across the group. "Why would you be more scared of the Jokers than you are of me?"

"That isn't the right question," the King explained. "The Jokers serve as the Queen's executioners. I've never known them to leave the castle grounds."

"What's your point?"

"Why would the Queen release the Jokers into the woods at all?"

It took Douglas a moment to understand what the King was implying.

"Because they were given different orders than you and your men here..."

The soldier responded with a solemn nod.

Douglas checked the ammunition in his gun before returning it to his waistband. "You win," he said. "Tell your men we're going back to see the Queen."

CHAPTER 18

AFTER ESCAPING THE flame-filled house, everyone crossed the yard to a small garden near the tree line. Once there, they huddled together beneath a rose bush so they would go unseen by anyone who might happen by.

"Is everyone okay?" one of the black bishops asked.

A wave of murmured replies passed through the group.

Finally catching her breath, Tay began searching the garden for Randy. Most of their companions had collapsed into the dirt. Many of the chess pieces had sustained injuries in their escape, their wooden bodies charred in spots where the flames had gotten a little too close.

Eventually Taylor found Randy standing near the garden's border with Father Mouse. Both were watching the cottage burn. It was only forty feet away, but it looked like a country mile from their perspective. On the horizon, what remained of the cabin was as large as a mountain in their eyes. The cabin smoldered, but the blaze was dying out at last. The fiery monster had eaten all it could and had left nothing behind but a blackened skeleton blanketed in soot and ash.

"Are you okay?" Taylor asked.

Randy kept his eyes fixed on the cottage. "How's Alice going to make it into Wonderland now? One world after another, he just keeps tearing them down."

Tay watched Randy with sad eyes. She didn't know what to say but realized she shouldn't press Randy to talk about his father.

Some wounds are better left alone.

"We'll need a headcount," Adrienne said. "We need to make sure everyone is accounted for. We can't leave anyone behind."

"What do you mean?" a pawn asked. "Where do you suggest we go?"

Adrienne gestured to the cabin. "Our home is no more. We can sit here and mourn our loss, or we can begin our search for a new board to call our own."

"We barely made it from the cottage to this garden. Now we're supposed to venture into the forest? The whole set will be dead by morning."

Others agreed with the pawn, their silence enough to let Adrienne know they wanted no part in her plan to leave the garden.

Taylor moved to join the discussion. "We'll help you," she said.

Randy turned. "Don't you think we have our own stuff to worry about?"

"We can't just leave them."

Tay expected Randy to shoot down the idea. That's what Wesley and Hope had done when she'd suggested something similar in Oz. Surely Randy would do the same. But even though she knew he wanted to protest, Randy never did. Instead, he silently gave in with a little nod.

Jezebel stepped to the front of the group. "What would you have us do, young lady? Just... wait here... hoping you'll eventually return?"

"For a while, yes. It's too dangerous for you in the forest. But if we can find a way to get big again, Randy and I can help you to find a new home."

"But how will you regain your size? All of the cakes and drinks have been destroyed in the fire."

"It's a big world out there. I'm sure there's something else we can eat."

"Perhaps I can be of some assistance."

The new voice came from deep within the garden's shadows, each of the words dragging out longer than they should. They sounded heavy, as if whomever had spoken them was struggling to say them at all.

Still on horseback, one of the knights pulled forward and drew his wooden sword. "Who goes there? Step forward and show yourself."

The unseen stranger blew smoke from the shadows before crawling into the light. "There's no need to arm yourself, good knight. I mean you no harm."

The children watched with the chess pieces as a fuzzy caterpillar slowly crawled from the darkness.

Its belly was colored like the ocean. His nose was a deep blue that matched the fur on its back. The caterpillar had three sets of pink hands and was using them to carry a brass hookah that allowed him to smoke from a pipe.

"It's you," Taylor said excitedly. "You're... you're the caterpillar."

"That's hardly true," the caterpillar explained. "I'm *a* caterpillar. To suggest I'm *the* caterpillar would be to suggest I'm the only one. Is that what you're trying to say, little girl?"

Taylor was taken aback by the snooty response.

"Now you know how I feel," he muttered.

"I only meant that you're the caterpillar who helped Alice when she—"

The blue bug raised up, throwing himself forward so he loomed over Taylor. *"I will not be accused of such things! Take it back! Take it back this instant!"*

Taylor flinched at how quickly the caterpillar had gone from grogginess to anger. But even as she prepared to defend herself, the caterpillar took a puff from his hookah and seemed to forget he was angry at all.

"Tell me, girl, what is your name?"

"Well... I'm... I'm Taylor."

"Of course you are. What a stupid name! I don't understand why your kind insists on such foolish names. Taylor, Alice – they mean nothing at all."

Growing agitated, Randy stepped into the bug's line-of-sight. "Dude?"

"What language does the boy speak?"

"A language all his own, believe me."

"Someone should tell him a language like that is useless to him."

"I'll do that," Taylor said.

"I don't see how," the caterpillar said. "He speaks his own language. He won't understand a word you say."

Tay sighed. "You said you might be able to help us?"

"I did, didn't I."

"Okay... would you mind telling us how?"

The caterpillar took a long drag from his hookah then blew smoke into the air. "You do remind me of her. Tell me: will I be persecuted for helping you the way people in Wonderland have been persecuted for aiding Alice."

"It's possible," Taylor said.

This brought a toothless grin to the caterpillar's face. "Good," he said. "I can't stand the Queen, all that yelling and screaming to cover up for the fact her bulbous head is an empty vessel. It's uncivilized."

The chess pieces chattered with excitement.

"You'll find everything you need near the Great Wall."

"Where's the Great Wall?" Randy asked.

The caterpillar fixed Randy with a confused look. "It's a great journey from here. And unfortunately for you, what you require often disappears in the morning light."

"What are you talking about?" Taylor asked.

The caterpillar yawned, his eyelids drooping like they might close at any moment. "Mushrooms, of course. You'll find them growing at the base of the Wall. But be cautious – eat from one side of the mushroom and you'll grow back to your normal size in no time; eat from the other and you'll shrink even more."

"Wait a minute," Randy said. "We can't get any smaller. If we shrink more than we already have..."

The caterpillar grinned. "You'll disappear like a candle's flame in the wind."

CHAPTER 19

FINDING TAYLOR WASN'T nearly as difficult as Wes thought it would be.

Sitting in the Archives Room, he and The Librarian had organized the library's oldest texts so they could search for any changes to their stories – changes similar to those they'd seen in Baum's book after their initial trip into Oz.

Soon after they began, Wes was stunned to find a book he didn't recognize in the pile. He knew the author, of course. Even if readers don't know his name, most know Lewis Carroll's most famous creation: *Alice in Wonderland*. But this title was new to Wesley. And while there was a remote possibility that he didn't know about this entry in the Wonderland series, he didn't think he would forget such an ominous title: *The Queen's Revenge*.

Wes fanned through the book's pages. He knew this was the clue they were after; that eventually he would stumble across a passage with Taylor's name or–

His heart stopped. He stared down at a half-page illustration of Taylor being chased by playing-card soldiers through the woods.

He'd found her. Tay was in Wonderland.

It was only on closer inspection that he noticed Randy was with her.

A lump raised in Wesley's throat. Why was Randy being chased? That didn't make sense. Wesley felt his face flush as a number of possibilities began to run through his head. Was Randy helping Taylor? Had they become friends again?

He pushed the ridiculous thought from his mind and began scanning the book's text for some kind of clarification. Anything that would let him know what was really going on. Wesley became so engrossed in his search that he didn't realize The Librarian was now watching over his shoulder.

"Have you found something?"

Startled, Wesley pushed to his feet, fidgeting with the heavy book as he handed it over. "I think I found them. They're in Wonderland. At least, they were."

The Librarian began thumbing through the tome. "It's off-putting to see Captain Hook and his men marching through Wonderland. Wouldn't you agree?"

Wes hadn't even noticed Hook appeared in a number of the book's illustrations. He was too caught up trying to answer questions of his own.

"Look here," the old man instructed.

The Librarian sat down at the table so they could look through the book together. He had stopped at a page a little more than halfway through the book. Strangely, it was here that the book's text came to an abrupt halt. Two-thirds of the page was blank. Upon closer inspection, Wesley understood why. Somehow, new words were appearing on the page one letter at a time as if an invisible typewriter was working away to help the author's story march down the page.

"What's going on?" Wesley asked.

"We've stumbled upon our first bit of luck. The story is rewriting itself."

"I thought we didn't want that to happen?"

"We don't," The Librarian began, "but this will make your friend much easier to find. We can use the book to trace her whereabouts as we venture into Wonderland after her."

Wesley liked the sound of that. Tay wouldn't have to pretend to like Randy for very much longer. He'd be there to get her soon.

"Oh my," the old man said.

Wes saw the old man had begun leafing through the book again. "What's wrong?" he asked.

"I believe Hook and the Queen are turning against Douglas..."

"Serves him right," Wesley smirked.

"Perhaps. But I'm worried it could further endanger your friends."

Wesley's jaw clenched. He didn't like the way The Librarian had referred to Randy and Taylor as his friends. Tay was his friend...

Randy was someone he had to deal with.

"We should get moving. First things first, however." The Librarian rose to his feet. "There's something you'll need if we're to save your friends."

"What's that?" Wesley asked.

"A staff."

CHAPTER 20

AT THEIR NORMAL size, Randy and Taylor could have covered ground much more quickly. Instead, their search for the Great Wall took most of the night. Making matters worse, both felt like they were trekking through a prehistoric land where everything was exponentially bigger than normal...

At one point they happened upon a puddle that blocked their path. Ordinarily, they could have hopped the puddle with ease. Instead, it was an obstacle that took thirty minutes for them to walk around.

Later, an army of fire ants sensed their presence and chased them through a muddy marsh. Back home those ants would have been little threat at all. But in Wonderland, at an inch tall, the red bugs were monsters that could have snapped either of the children in two.

That's how most of their evening progressed. It made for a distressing night. And yet, as they pushed through a low-hanging fog, Tay couldn't help but notice something else had changed since their escape from the Queen. Sure, they were fighting to survive in Wonderland. But Randy and Taylor were no longer fighting each other. An easiness was growing between them. As if they had weathered a devastating storm, and this was the calm that followed.

Eventually the sun made its first appearance from beneath the horizon, blessing Wonderland with warmth just as the exhausted children finally happened upon the Great Wall. Wary after so many close calls, both treated it like a mirage that had materialized to trick them. It was only after they got close enough to touch the structure that either allowed themselves to feel any real relief.

Made of collected stones, the wall was just four feet tall. But to them, in their current state, it might as well have been a thousand.

"I can't believe we finally made it," Randy explained.

Taylor pointed to something just down the path. "I know. Look."

The kids hurried along the base of the towering wall toward a patch of mushrooms growing in a soggy area of mud and grass.

"There," Tay continued, "just like the Caterpillar said."

Standing four or five times the children's height, each of the mushrooms had a long, white stalk that extended upward from the mud until it reached a broad, circular cap. The undersides of the caps were milky white and ribbed like gills on a fish. Their tops were red with yellow polka dots.

"I didn't think they'd be that big," Randy said.

"It's because we're so small."

"I know that. It's just: what are we supposed to

do now?"

"Well, we can chop one down... which would take forever; or... we can *climb*."

Taylor bolted for the mushroom patch, running so fast her ponytail bounced back-and-forth behind her.

"You're really gonna climb that thing?" Randy hollered.

"I'll bring you some down if you're scared."

Randy's mouth turned up in disgust. "Oh! Really?"

The boy sprinted after her. Taylor laughed when they reached the dark sludge that covered the base of the mushroom patch. Randy's happiness came to a screeching halt when he saw his sneakers sink into the mud.

"Ugh! Are you serious right now?"

"Boys worry more about their shoes than girls, I swear."

Randy launched himself forward so he could wrap his arms around the mushroom's stalk, dig in his feet, and begin to climb. When he did, Randy landed so his face was flush against the plant's soft stem. He immediately pulled away in disgust. "Good luck! This thing is covered in slime. And... it stinks! Jeez!"

His running jump had left him just high enough that Tay had to look up at him. "It's a mushroom, Randy. What did you think it was going to smell like: daisies?"

"You should probably be a little nicer," Randy

suggested.

"Yeah? Why's that?"

"Maybe I'll keep all the 'shrooms for myself. Maybe I won't let you get big again. When I'm back to normal, maybe I'll carry you around in my pocket like a pet. I mean: it's not like you could climb this thing for real even if you tried."

"I'm gonna do better than that," she said. "I'm gonna *beat* you to the top."

Randy laughed it off until he saw just how quickly Taylor was able to scale the mushroom.

"Wait a minute!"

When Tay didn't answer, Randy finally started to move.

They were halfway up the mushroom stalks before either said another word.

"Mine's taller than yours," Randy complained. "And you got a head start."

"Keep those excuses ready."

"Shut up!"

Side by side, the kids climbed. Each enjoyed the moment – no doubt relieved to have some time that didn't require them to run for their lives. They continued upward, laughing and fussing as they became covered in the mushrooms' slimy residue. By the time they reached the mushroom caps, the race was even.

Instinctively, Randy tapped the underside of the cap just as he would tap the ceiling after climbing the rope in gym. "First."

"I thought we were racing to the top?"

From Randy's perspective, the mushroom cap looked like a twelve-foot overhang with no clear handholds and a twenty-foot drop to the ground below.

"It's not like we can go any farther," he said.

"Please," Taylor mocked. "*You* can't."

Tay forced her hand into the soft flesh of the cap's belly. She made sure she had a firm grip; that the improvised handhold would support her weight. Then, when she saw it would, Taylor eased her body forward.

"What are you doing? Don't!"

Tay released her off-hand and freed her feet so they dangled beneath her. Her eyes widened when she felt the pull of gravity, only then realizing she'd put all her faith in her ability to hold onto the slimy mushroom with a single hand.

"Okay, so this wasn't the best idea!"

"No kidding," Randy said. "Just go back."

Taylor shook her head then lunged forward, shoving her free hand into toadstool's flesh so she had twice the grip.

"Dude! Stop!"

Taylor traversed the toadstool's overhang one hand at a time, her feet kicking the entire way. When she reached the cap's edge, Tay got a good grip with both hands then swung her feet forward. Sure she had enough momentum to carry her the rest of the way, Taylor let go and flipped over the edge of the toadstool so she landed safely atop the mushroom's cap.

All Randy could do was gape at her, mouth hanging open in disbelief.

Taylor rose to her feet. The mushroom swayed beneath her weight. She had to fight for balance until she made it to the mushroom's center and took a seat. "You coming?" she prodded.

Randy nervously sized up his own route to the top before moving to follow Taylor's lead. Although hesitant, he did fine, eventually pulling himself up so he could throw a leg over the edge and crawl onto the top of the mushroom. Then, just as Taylor had before him, he stood on wobbly legs until he found balance at the center of the mushroom and sat down.

Looking over, a cocky grin split Taylor's face.

"What?" Randy asked, still catching his breath.

"I wanna hear you say it."

"Say what?"

"Who won?"

Randy looked away to hide a smile of his own. "You did."

"That means you have to take the first bite, right?"

Randy scrunched up his face in disgust. "No!"

"Maybe we should do it together," she suggested.

Tay dug her fingers into the mushroom's colorful cap and pulled a fistful of the plant's flesh free. After seeing her do it, Randy did the same.

Taylor sniffed the handful of pulp then recoiled with her nose in the air. "No way! I can't do it. I don't even like mushrooms on my pizza."

Randy touched the tip of his tongue to the mushroom and pulled away even faster than Taylor had. "We'll do it together, okay?"

Taylor answered with a nod.

"One, two—"

Randy was just about to pop the bite into his mouth when Taylor stopped him.

"Wait!"

Randy rolled his eyes. "I'm trying to eat my vegetables here."

"How do we know we're eating from the right side?"

Randy pulled the bite away from his mouth. "I forgot all about that."

"Me too," Taylor said. "What happens if we shrink like the Caterpillar said? We'll be too small to do anything. It sounds like we'll just... disappear."

Randy gave this some concerned thought. "I guess that's up to you."

"What's that supposed to mean?"

"You'll have to find a way to save me if this doesn't work."

Randy threw the mushroom into his mouth without another word. Color drained from Tay's face. She watched in terror as Randy chewed the bite, threw his head back and swallowed. When it was gone, he quickly threw another bite into his mouth. Then another.

"Not so much!" Not so much!"

But Randy ate the whole thing. Every bite. When he was finished, he even licked the stink off his palms for good measure.

"Oh man!" he exclaimed. "Are you seeing this?"

Randy's torso thinned until it looked like a stretched piece of chewing gum. Tay was sure he would snap right in half. But he didn't. Instead, his body quickly added weight as the rest of him grew.

When she saw he would be okay, Taylor bit down on her own mushroom. Her metamorphosis began even quicker than his.

The two of them watched in awe as the world shrunk around them. Trees pulled down from the heavens, trunks shortening so their tops could be seen by the kids once more. The mushrooms they sat upon shrank until they were crushed beneath the children's weight. It happened to everything around them. The world was shrinking. At least, that's how it felt to them.

But of course, it was the children who were changing, not the world around them. They were morphing back to their normal selves.

When it was over, Randy and Tay stood near the Great Wall, but now the structure only came to their chests and didn't seem so great at all. In fact, both were stunned to realize their night-long journey had not taken them very far at all. The smoldering carcass of the cottage was just a few hundred yards away...

The Great Wall sat on the border of the home's property.

"You have got to be kidding me," Randy said.

Randy's disgust made Taylor laugh. A moment

later, they were giggling together. They'd pushed themselves to exhaustion to make it this far. Now they could return to the cottage garden in just a few minutes.

"Well," Taylor began, "at least we won't have to go far to find the others."

Randy was about to respond when something moved in the darkness behind them. It sounded like an animal's feet – paws shuffling through fallen leaves.

Whatever it was, it was heading their way.

The kids turned. Both checked the stone wall in front of them, realizing it would offer little protection if they were under attack again.

But they didn't have to live with that dark thought long. In fact, they weren't sure what to think when they saw the familiar face step from the shadows.

Randy shook his head like he didn't believe his eyes at all.

"Bates?"

CHAPTER 21

"DUDE!" RANDY EXCLAIMED. "You've got a staff, too? Sweet!"

Taylor's shock turned to confusion when she got a good look at Wesley. Her eyes moved from his chiseled staff to his dirty and tattered clothes. His body was covered in fresh scabs and purple bruises. It seemed Wes had been through even more of an ordeal than their own. He looked older too, as if years had passed instead of days. Of course, none of that mattered to Tay. She didn't care where Wes had been, how he'd gotten there or why – all that mattered to her was that she was finally being reunited with her friend.

"Wes," she began, tears welling, "what are you doing here?"

Without warning, Wesley leapt onto the wall so he was standing over Randy. He swung his staff in a furious arc at Randy's head. Randy did his best to block the attack, cowering with both arms raised for protection. The blow was still enough to knock him to the ground.

Taylor couldn't believe it. *"Wesley! What are you doing?"*

"What are *you* doing? Run!"

"What? No!"

Wesley looked to The Librarian. *"Get her out of here!"*

Recovering nearby, Randy muttered something beneath his breath. Wesley hopped down from the wall and prepared to swing his staff again. This time Taylor grabbed Wesley's arm before he could.

"Stop it!" she exclaimed. "You don't understand! Things... are different."

Confusion creased Wesley's brow.

"Perhaps we should give them a chance to explain," The Librarian suggested.

Taylor stepped between the boys. "He helped me escape, Wes."

"I know... we saw... but... I thought... I thought you were just using him."

"You think I would do that?" Taylor asked.

Wes stared at her without answering.

"What do you mean you saw?" Randy asked.

Wesley dug through The Librarian's satchel. He pulled out *The Queen's Revenge* and shoved it into Randy's hand. "I know you're not big on reading, but you should give this one a try. Really."

This time Randy made a move toward Wes like he was ready to fight. The Librarian lowered his staff between them.

"See that?" Wesley barked. "He hasn't changed. He can't wait to put his hands on me!"

"Stop yelling at her!" Randy shouted. "You're mad at me, not her."

Wes looked to Taylor. "You saw that, right?"

"You just hit him in the head," Taylor reminded.

Wes felt his chest seize up. He was eye-to-eye with the bully who had made his life miserable every day since his move to Astoria. Randy was the bad guy. And yet, everyone was determined to treat Wesley like *he* was the one out-of-line.

"Where's your father?" The Librarian asked Randy.

"I think he's gone back to the Queen's castle."

The Librarian's worry was obvious.

"Why?" Randy asked. "What's wrong?"

"We're worried Hook and the Queen may be turning against him."

"Are you serious? Then we've got to get moving. We've got to go help him!"

Wesley responded before anyone else could. "We're here to bring Taylor home. You can do whatever you want." He turned to face Taylor like he expected her to follow him back into the woods.

"We can't just leave Randy here to fend for himself," Taylor said.

"Why not?"

No one was sure how to respond to Wesley's hot-tempered tone.

"What? Am I supposed to forget everything he's done? You know how he is: he'll act like your best friend; next thing you know, he's super-gluing your face to the floor."

Taylor passed her attention back-and-forth between the two boys, unsure how to move forward when strange sounds filtered through the shadows towards them—

Clickety-clack, clickety clack.

"Now what the heck is that?" Randy asked nervously.

"I'm not sure I know," The Librarian answered.

The wind picked up as the chattering disturbance grew louder, closing in.

Click-clack, clickety clack.

The long shadows of the forest began to move as two dark figures stepped into view. Neither was easy to make out in the haze, but the kids could see the strangers were playing-card men. Still, there was something different about these two. The men watching them now wore black top hats. The kids could tell they had thin arms and gaunt faces, but it was only when one of them stepped into a shaft of light filtering through the trees that the children understood why.

"Oh my god," Taylor whispered.

The Joker's face had no eyes or skin to speak of. No lips or ears. All that remained of a nose was a dark cavity in the center of the stranger's face. Even his lanky arms gleamed in the light, nothing but white bone where muscle and tendon should have been.

The Librarian tightened his grip on his staff. "No one move."

The Joker leaned forward, his paper body contorting into an arch so he could stand on all-fours. His head shifted so it was parallel to the ground. The sunken voids where his eyes should have been stared out at them. Then, as if signaling his companion, the Joker struck his teeth together with a familiar...

Click-clack. Clack, clack, clack.

The second Joker sprang from the shadows. Top hat in hand, he spiraled his body to create momentum then threw his hat at the group like a frisbee.

"Get down!" The Librarian yelled.

The old man and Taylor dove into the dirt. Randy was about to follow their lead when he saw Wes frozen in place. Their attacker was still looking at him with the same slanted stare. Wesley seemed to be locked in some strange staring contest with their skeletal attacker. He couldn't look away.

"Bates! Man, move!"

Lunging forward, Randy tackled Wesley to the ground just in time to let the hat whistle by. While it may have missed its mark, the hat's razor-sharp brim tore through a nearby tree like a doctor's saw cutting through bone.

All four rose to their feet, staring in disbelief as the tree slowly fell to earth.

Stunned, Taylor was the first to say a word. "Umm... what?!"

The lethal hat was now arcing on a return path to its owner. Wes wheeled about just in time to see the first attacker catch it in one of his boney hands.

Click-clack, clickety-clack.

Randy looked to The Librarian beside him. "Please tell me you can fight these things with that staff. Call down some fireballs or something."

"For the moment, I suggest we try something else."

"What?" Taylor asked.

"I suggest we run."

With that, the old man took up his staff and retreated into the forest.

"Here we go again," Randy smirked.

The kids sprinted after The Librarian just as the Jokers reeled back to fire their bladed hats once more. And this time, when the weapons were away, the Jokers moved to pursue their prey.

Wesley and The Librarian dodged one of the hats just in time to watch it whiz between them. Its blade caught the old man's arm so a blood stain bloomed on his sleeve. Behind them, Randy and Tay leapt into a small gulley and let the hat intended for them pass overhead.

The kids got to their feet and started running again. All three quickly pulled ahead of the old man. At first, Wes thought it was because The Librarian's old bones wouldn't allow him to move that fast.

But then the Jokers let their weapons fly again...

The hats whistled as they cut down everything in their paths: brush, branches, vines and overgrowth. Nothing survived. And all the time, the whistle grew louder as the hats closed in. When the high-pitched scream was nearly enough to make their ears bleed, The Librarian spun around and drove his staff into the dirt.

"Obice!"

The yellow stone atop his staff glowed white-hot. A wall of yellow light extended outward from his staff in both directions. The barrier was enough to block the whistling hats and send them into the dirt.

"Did you see that?" Randy exclaimed.

That's how the chase unfolded for the next several minutes. The Jokers would send their hats spinning after them, only to watch helplessly as The Librarian used his magic to bat them away.

But by the time they broke through the tree line, the old man didn't look like he would be able to defend them much longer. In fact, when the kids stopped to assess the rocky hillside ahead of them, The Librarian had to lean on Randy for support.

Wesley pointed to a narrow pathway between jagged cliffs just a few hundred feet away. "We'll head for that ridge. Do you think you can make it?"

Drained, the old man answered with an unconvincing nod.

Click-clack.

All four looked into the forest.

"If we don't make it to the ridge before they come out of the woods..."

Taylor didn't finish her thought.

Wes scanned the area, looking for any hope of an easy escape. Instead his attention fell on a small cave burrowed just beneath the ridge line.

"We'll have to find a better way," he explained.

Wesley put an arm around the old man and started up the rocky hillside. Randy and Tay shared a nervous look before moving along the same route.

All the while, the Jokers closed.
Clickety-clack.
Click...
Clack.

CHAPTER 22

THEY REACHED THE cave just in time to avoid being seen when the Jokers came into view. Once inside, Wesley helped The Librarian to a seat on the cave's dirt floor. The rusted remains of fallen armor and weapons littered the ground all around them. Stripped of flesh, bones formed a trail into the darkness beyond the cave's entrance. Wes studied the trail with a look of concern as Randy and Tay positioned themselves so they could watch what was happening outside.

The Jokers had scaled the rocky incline and were now looking about in confusion. One clacked his teeth in disapproval then leapt from one boulder to the next on his way toward the forest below.

But the other sensed something was amiss...

He craned his neck, looking back in the kids' direction.

When his sunken eyes fell on the cave his spine straightened, cracking so loudly that Randy and Tay could hear it from thirty yards away.

"Oh crap," Randy whispered.

"What is it?" Wesley asked.

"He knows..."

Wes hurried over for a look. The Joker was summersaulting his way up the hillside, his body bending and contorting the whole way. Somehow it was even more unsettling than the Joker's lifeless appearance, like watching a Slinky come alive to *climb* a staircase.

"We'll lose him in the cave," Wesley suggested.

Randy motioned to the discarded armor and bones. "Really? This isn't some empty cave waiting to be explored."

"What exactly do you think we're going to find?"

"I know what we're going to find!" He looked to Tay for confirmation.

"The Jabberwock," she whispered.

Wesley looked at her sideways.

"We heard the soldiers talking about it before."

Their attacker would reach the cave's entrance in a matter of moments.

Randy gestured to Wesley's staff. "Can you do anything with that thing?"

Instinctively, Wesley put the staff behind his back. "I don't know. Maybe."

"Maybe's not going to get it done, Bates."

"We've got rocks," Taylor said. "Rocks and a lot of cover."

Everyone looked over as The Librarian rose to his feet. "If you'll step back, I can handle this." He started toward them but stumbled forward when he was no longer able to lean on the wall for support. Wesley and Tay hurried over to catch him before he fell into the dirt.

Randy rolled his eyes. "We're a real group of all-stars, huh?"

"We're open to ideas," Wesley snapped.

After a moment's thought, Randy took a deep breath. "I could give myself up."

Taylor looked up with a start. "What? No! No way. They'll kill you."

"Maybe not."

"You didn't like *my* maybe," Wesley reminded.

"They want me so they can get to my dad."

"So they'll kill you later instead of killing you now? Sounds like a great plan."

"It is if they let the two of you go."

Wes was so taken aback by Randy's willingness to sacrifice himself he wasn't sure how to respond. In the end, Taylor did before he could...

"They're after us both, Randy."

Randy closed his eyes. "I know."

"Forget it!" Wesley exclaimed. "No! I–"

Taylor cut him off. "You know it's the only way, Wes."

Wesley's frustration suddenly felt like a tidal wave crashing down on him. "I... no... I just found you..."

She smiled. "That was the easy part. Now you've got to save me."

❖ ❖ ❖

As soon as they stepped from the cave, Wesley hid in the shadows so he could watch as the Joker approached Randy and Tay. His stomach knotted. Intuition told him the plan wasn't going to work.

He grabbed his staff but knew there wasn't much he could do if things went south. If the Joker wanted them dead, Randy and Tay would be gone before Wes had a chance to react.

"Easy," The Librarian instructed. "Patience."

The Joker immediately shoved Randy and Taylor into the gravel at their feet.

Clack-clack, the Joker called. *Clack. Clack. Clack.*

A moment later, the second attacker reappeared.

Sight of the captured children seemed to irritate the second Joker. He click-clacked an argument to his companion then turned his attention to the kids.

Wesley held his breath as the Joker snatched Taylor by the shirt and yanked her to her feet. He shoved her down the hill and gestured toward the forest with one of his skeletal hands.

Click-clack. Click-clack.

Taylor shot the Joker a puzzled look. When she didn't respond, the Joker shoved her down the incline again. This time, she did fall, skinning both knees.

Randy sprang to his feet. *"Dude! Stop!"*

Thinking the boy would better understand, the Joker pushed Randy down the hill then made the same gesture toward the tree line.

"They want them to run," The Librarian whispered.

"Why?"

"They love the chase."

The Jokers continued harassing Randy and Tay until it became painfully obvious to both that the children would not comply with their demands. Then each of the frustrated Jokers grabbed one of the children and began leading them down the hill.

Satisfied, Wesley turned to face The Librarian. "It worked!"

"Indeed. They've done their part. Now it's time to do ours."

Wes nodded in agreement. He knew the challenges before them were great, but somewhere inside, Wesley knew they would prevail...

They'd found a way to storm the castle in Oz.

They'd traveled across worlds to find Tay.

They'd already done the impossible.

They could do it again. They—

Click-clack.

A chill turned Wesley's spine to ice. He turned to see one of the Jokers was standing just outside the cave's entrance. The assassin was already corkscrewing to throw his hat. No time to spare, Wes bolted for cover behind a boulder just as the Joker released his weapon.

But the hat wasn't traveling a path toward Wesley. It wasn't coming for the older man either. Instead, the Joker had trained his sights on something else.

Wes looked up just in time to see the weapon's blade cut a section of earth free from the overhead ridge. The canopy gave way so a curtain of giant rocks and gravel fell down on Wes.

"Go!" The Librarian shouted.

Wesley didn't listen.

Holding his ground, Wes lifted his staff into the air and spoke a command he'd heard the old man speak several times before.

"Obice!"

Wesley had spoken in a deep voice that wasn't quite his own. When he did, the stone atop his staff came alive with light. Wes might have conjured that light into something more, but the cave-in didn't give him a chance. Instead, the stone's light was extinguished in a wave of falling rock and dirt, and Wesley's world went black.

CHAPTER 23

HOPE STOOD WAITING just outside the castle's entrance as Douglas returned with the Queen's men. She allowed the playing-card soldiers to march past her. Their synchronized steps echoed through the building's grand foyer until they disappeared down a long corridor. When they were finally gone, Hope joined Douglas near the gate.

"I thought I told you to keep an eye on things," Douglas said.

Hope recoiled at his brusque tone. "I'm sorry. But I saw you coming from the tower. I wanted to hear what happened."

"I'm sorry. I found them, but it's complicated. Randy wouldn't come back, and things escalated from there. Did you know the Queen sent more soldiers after we left?"

"I'm not sure it was the Queen."

"What do you mean?"

"It's Hook. He's different. It's like the longer he's away from Neverland..."

"The more dangerous he becomes."

She nodded a reply.

"None of this is going the way it was supposed to."

Hope grinned. "Things rarely do."

"And sometimes they're doomed from the start."

Her smile fell. "What are you saying?"

A grave look clouded Douglas's face. "I don't know."

◆ ◆ ◆

Wesley's ears rang, the air around him thick with dust.

Fighting a cough, The Librarian muttered something and the stone atop his staff emitted a warm glow to push the darkness into the far corners of the cave.

The old man had been standing at a safe-enough distance that he'd not been in immediate danger during the cave-in, but now he was moving closer to inspect just how precarious their situation had become. He tested a few of the fallen stones with his staff, but truthfully, just a glance at the blocked entrance had told him everything he needed to know...

The rockslide had sealed the pair inside the cave.

Wesley picked himself off the ground. "I... I tried to stop it."

"It was a noble effort.'

"Will we be able to get out?"

A crooked grin lit the old man's face. "Not the way we hoped."

"I don't understand," Wesley said. "Why are you smiling?"

"The plan was sound. The Jokers should have left

us alone once they apprehended your friends. Unless..."

"Unless?"

The Librarian moved past the fallen armor on his way deeper into the cave. "Unless they were *supposed* to help us."

Confused, Wesley hurried after him. "Umm, that didn't feel like help to me. I'm pretty sure they were trying to kill us."

"Oh, I'm sure that was in their minds. But you remember how you felt in Oz? The way the world seemed to open up just enough to guide you on your journey? As if an unseen hand was pushing you in the right direction?"

"I guess..."

"Who's to say we aren't experiencing that same thing now. After all, there's now but one path for us to follow."

Wesley looked down at the discarded human bones scattered across the cave's floor. "I wonder if these guys felt the same way."

"I trust Wonderland to provide a solution for every challenge we face."

"How can you be so sure?"

The Librarian's smile grew. "She did for Alice; she'll do it for us too."

❖ ❖ ❖

The Jokers dragged Randy and Taylor through a network of dank passageways buried beneath the castle. After a series of twists and turns, they eventually happened upon a long corridor. Lit torches lined one side of the hall. Barred prison cells were spaced evenly opposite the torches.

The Jokers shoved Randy and Tay into one of the empty cells then slammed the door shut behind them before disappearing back down the hall. The kids were only beginning to get their bearings when a familiar voice greeted them from the shadows of a neighboring cell.

"Why – I remember you."

The Hatter's hands were wrapped around two of the bars separating his cell from theirs.

"Awful way to spend one's unbirthday, wouldn't you say?"

"You can say that again," Taylor answered.

The Hatter furrowed his brow. "Of course I can. But... weren't you listening?"

"No... I was... it's just... forget it." Taylor trudged over to a tiny window for a look at the castle's courtyard.

"Have you tried to escape?" Randy asked.

"Oh no," the Hatter began, "we will when it's appropriate to do so, but there are more pressing matters at hand."

"Like what?"

The March Hare leapt from the shadows. "We're out of tea!"

The frazzled Hare held out his empty tea cup in a trembling hand.

"Is that the girl who got us into this mess?"

This new voice belonged to a woman in a cell at the end of the hall.

"No. She isn't Alice." The Hare looked over at Tay. "You aren't, are you?"

Taylor shook her head.

"You'll have to excuse the Duchess. She's a bit of a grump."

"I am not! I just miss that bawling baby of mine."

The Hatter stepped aside so the kids could see into the cell beyond theirs. Seated alone in her cell, the Duchess's face was wrinkled like a prune. Her head was twice as large as a normal head and ended in a sharp point at her chin.

"Are you Friends of Alice?" the Hare asked.

"No," Taylor explained. "We've never met her."

This left the Hatter perplexed. "Then why are you here?"

"It's a long story," Randy said.

"I assure you, it's not as complicated as you believe."

Everyone turned their attention toward this new voice.

The kids had forgotten all about the cell behind them. Somehow, they'd missed the mystical beast that was locked away there.

So large Randy wondered how it had gotten into the dungeon at all, the gryphon had the body of a lion and the head of an eagle. Its claws ended in long talons. When it got to its feet and started their way, Tay saw the ceiling was so low the gryphon was unable to stretch its wings.

"We've all been sentenced to this grave existence for the same reason."

The gryphon spoke in a voice that sounded both old and wise.

"Why's that?" Taylor asked.

"Because the world's gone mad! Things have changed since we fell under the Queen's rule. Reasoned thought no longer exists in Wonderland. Anyone who questions things; anyone who dares to be different; anyone who wants to try something new – they'll all suffer the same fate."

"Why do people let her get away with that?"

"What would you have them do?" the Hatter asked.

"Fight back?"

The gryphon lowered its head. "You'd be surprised how easy it is for people to look away as long as evil doesn't come for them."

"I don't believe that," Taylor said. "I don't believe that at all."

"Believe it or not, you're going to see firsthand soon enough."

◆ ◆ ◆

Wesley and The Librarian had discovered a labyrinth of rocky passageways and corridors deep within the mountain. At one point, Wes felt so turned around he was sure they'd never make it out; that they were destined to wander until their bones were added to the collection that littered the cave.

Then a dim light appeared at the end the long passage before them.

"Is that it?" Wesley asked.

"There's only one way to find out," The Librarian said.

As they got closer, golden light shimmered like sunlight bouncing off a still lake. It was only as they stepped into the ankle-deep water of the large cavern awaiting them that they understood why...

The open-air room soared to an opening in the rock nearly two-hundred feet above their heads. The trickle of a waterfall had likely formed the cavern over thousands of years, its water spilling into the room from the overhead ledge. But it was not the reflection of sunlight off the water that had created the golden shimmer that had caught their eye; it was the reflection of light off the mountain of treasure piled in the center of the room.

"Are you kidding me?" Wesley exclaimed. *"Look at that! Look!"*

Gold coins and jewelry, mammoth jewels and stringed pearls, ornate eggs encrusted with diamonds. Anything one could imagine was hidden away in the mountain. It was like someone had collected all of Wonderland's treasure and dropped it through the open roof above. It was the stuff of legend, the kind of treasure often spoken of – but never found.

"We're rich! I'm mean: holy cow, dude. We are rich!"

"I'd lower my voice."

The Librarian lifted his gaze. Wesley followed the old man's line-of-sight until his own eyes fell on what had captured The Librarian's interest.

"Okay," Wesley muttered. "We're dead. We're so dead."

Big as a house, a dragon was curled in a tight ball atop the treasure, eyes closed and lost in slumber.

"Is that—"

"The Jabberwock, I'm afraid."

"How are we supposed to get past that?" Wesley asked nervously.

The Librarian sat down to rest. "I was about to ask you that very question."

Wesley wasn't sure how to respond.

"Remember: there are no limits. Anything is possible."

Wes looked down at his feet. He didn't like the way this conversation was unfolding. It was starting to feel like a pop quiz, and this wasn't the time.

"I... I don't know. I can't think of anything."

The old man shook his head. "Still so worried what others will think."

Wesley looked up sharply. "Fine," he blurted. "I think we should—"

The Librarian raised a finger to his lips: a reminder to keep quiet.

"Neither one of us can climb these walls," Wesley whispered. "You're still recovering from before, and I'm not exactly known for my upper-body strength."

"Then what do we do?"

Wesley was so unsure of his answer that he wasn't sure he was willing to share it at all. "We fly?"

The old man arched an eyebrow. "Are you *asking* me; or are you *telling* me?"

"You've used light to block an avalanche and fight off the Queen's men," Wesley said. "Why can't you use it to lift us out of here?"

"Why can't *you*?"

"No way," Wesley protested. "I barely picked up those rocks. And you saw what happened when I tried to stop the cave-in before."

"Yes. You failed..."

Sensing Wesley's embarrassment, The Librarian got to his feet.

"Do you know what kind of people fail in a situation like that?"

Looking away, Wesley refused to answer.

"The best people. I don't care that you failed, Wesley. Life isn't won by those who get it right on their first attempt. It's won by those who see failure for what it is... one step closer to success."

Wes stayed quiet for a long moment before speaking.

"I wouldn't use light the way you do."

"How would you write our escape?"

Wesley looked up at the opening then shifted his attention to the water at their feet. It was only now that he noticed the cavern floor was covered in coins like the bottom of a wishing well.

"You'll want to get a little closer," he said. "I'm

not sure this will work."

The Librarian took a position beside Wesley just as the boy twirled his staff so he could put its crystal into the water at their feet.

Wes closed his eyes. He did his best to push any thought away except the one that mattered. Just then, the submerged crystal began to glow. A series of tiny air bubbles floated up from the floor. Hundreds. Thousands. More.

Eyes wide as he watched Wesley work, The Librarian let his gaze fall on a bubble that seemed to be growing bigger than the rest.

It floated toward them, refusing to pop when it reached the surface as the others had. The pocket of air didn't even burst when it touched the old man's leg. Instead, it pushed through his presence, slowly sealing him and Wes inside its growing sphere. And when it had grown large enough to encapsulate them both—

The bubble lifted them into the air.

Stunned, the old man watched as they pulled away from the floor, the cavern walls whipping past them as they picked up speed toward the ceiling.

Beside him, Wesley kept his eyes shut. After his failure in Oz, he felt just one look would be enough to break his concentration. And the higher they got, the more dangerous any fall became. Plus, they might wake the Jabberwock...

Thoughts of the dragon had just entered his mind when the bubble burst.

Wes opened his eyes just as he and The Librarian began to fall.

Both slammed face first into the pile of treasure. While the impact hurt, the mountain of gold slowed their descent to the cavern floor. Together, they tumbled down the shimmering bank until they came to rest in the water below.

"Well," The Librarian groaned, "that wasn't bad for a first attempt."

"First attempt?" Wesley struggled to his feet. As if he wasn't feeling miserable enough, his clothes were now sopping wet. "I'm not doing that again."

"Wesley..."

"Why are you trying to train me now? Every minute you spend trying to teach me the 'ways of the Force' is a minute wasted, a minute Taylor doesn't have."

"And what happens if you need these skills to save her when the time comes?"

"What are you talking about? This *is* the time! Just get us out of here!"

The Librarian kept his attention fixed on the boy for a long moment before turning to look for his staff which had fallen into the water nearby. "I should remind you to keep your voice down so as not to wake the Jabberwock."

Wes could hear hurt in The Librarian's voice.

Or maybe it was disappointment.

"There it is!" The Librarian pulled his staff from the water then joined Wesley near the center of the room. "Now... if you'll step back..."

Whispering a spell, The Librarian conjured a magic carpet of light that floated just above the water nearby. The old man stepped onto the carpet then waited for Wesley to follow suit. When he was aboard, the carpet began to rise.

This time Wesley had every opportunity to watch as they flew toward the exit. He felt lighter than air as they picked up speed, moving alongside the mountain of gold then past the snoring dragon perched at its peak. When they left the cavern, Wesley had a view of Wonderland beyond compare...

The Fungal Forest took up an expanse at the base of the mountain range with its giant toadstools. Beyond that, the Pool of Tears remained from Alice's first foray into Wonderland. Quaint cottages dotted the landscape as far as the eye could see. Eventually they got high enough to see the Endless Sea on the horizon.

And sitting between them and the sea, was the Queen's castle.

Wonderland had led them in the right direction just as The Librarian predicted.

Wesley should have been elated. He was flying. He was *literally* flying.

And yet, he felt his heart sink.

Could he have gotten them out on his own? He'd been so close in his first attempt. If only he hadn't given up so easily, maybe *he* could have been the one to guide their magical flight. Why had he quit like that? The old man was right. Failure wasn't the worst thing in the world. He'd already gotten over that. Instead, all he felt now was regret, and he already tell it was something he was going to feel for a long time to come.

CHAPTER 24

DOUGLAS AND HOPE did not find the Queen in her chambers. By coincidence, she and Hook had convened on a tower balcony that offered the same view of Wonderland Wes and The Librarian were enjoying from their magic carpet.

Two guards stood on either side of doors that opened onto the balcony. When they saw Douglas storming their way, both lowered their spears across his path to prevent him from stepping through the archway.

"Let us pass," Douglas demanded.

Douglas pushed by the guards before either could respond. While tentative, Hope did the same. The Queen stepped forward to greet them.

"Back so soon," she said.

"What were your orders?" Douglas demanded.

The Queen's jaw clenched. "I beg your pardon."

"I told you those children weren't to be harmed. You were ordered—"

The Queen cut him short. "No one orders me to do anything. Not in Wonderland. Those who dare are the first to lose their heads!"

Hope looked over to see Smee was standing with three of Hook's men nearby. The pirates leered at Hope from the shadows. They looked like a pack of dogs drooling in anticipation of a few steaks being tossed their way.

"It's only your kingdom as long as I allow you to rule."

Standing nearby, Hook began to laugh.

"Is there something funny?" Douglas asked.

"I've never seen someone turn on his allies as quickly as you do. *And I'm a pirate!* If I didn't laugh, I'm afraid I might cry. After all, if you're turning on us now, who's to say you won't when we have helped you to get what you want? Who's to say you won't just toss us back into our cells and throw away the key?"

"I've given you my word," Douglas reminded. "I'm only here now because the Queen broke hers. Did you have something to do with that, captain?"

"It's possible," Hook responded. "Frankly, after your behavior in the courtyard, we'd both feel much happier if you would provide us with some form of insurance."

"I don't know what that means..."

"We'd like you to give us one of your amulets."

Douglas felt flush. He looked to Hope, only now realizing just how vulnerable their position was on the balcony like this.

"That's not going to happen," Douglas said.

Hook lifted the corner of his mouth into a half grin. Beside him, the Queen looked like she was about to break into a fit of laughter.

"But you haven't heard our offer to you," she said.

At this, Douglas could barely breath. These weren't smart people, but both of the villains were talking as if they'd already gotten the better of him.

Hook began to pace, his hand on the hilt of his sword. "It's so unlike me to take prisoners, but in your case, I'm afraid I had to make an exception."

"Wait," Hope began, "are you taking us prisoner?"

"He isn't talking about us. You've found the kids, haven't you?"

The Queen's smile grew.

"Where's my son?"

"First... the amulet."

Douglas shook his head in frustration. "Are you sure you want to do this? Free will carries consequences. There's no going back after this."

Hook drew his sword. "It could be worse," he explained. "We won't leave you trapped in a life without meaning the way the people in your world have imprisoned us. Give us just one of the amulets, and we'll free the children. Otherwise..." Hook gestured for the Queen to finish his thought.

"They'll lose their heads at sundown with everyone else."

The Queen's men had blocked the door. The pirates had stepped from the shadows so they were within striking distance.

"If only you could be this calculating in your battle against Pan."

Hook tightened his grip on his sword. "The amulet."

Douglas pulled the pistol from his waistband in

a flash, quickly leveling the weapon at Hook's head. His finger found the trigger and–

One of the Queen's soldiers brought a spear down on his outstretched arm just as Douglas squeezed off a shot. The blow forced his aim toward the floor so the bullet ricocheted off the marble tile. He immediately spun about, sure Hook's men had used the moment to get the drop on him. All three were right there, the tips of their swords coming together at Douglas's throat.

"Wait!" Hope shouted. *"I'll give you what you want."*

"Hope! No!"

Hope removed her necklace, revealing the engraved pendant that hung from its silk cord. She stepped toward Hook, hand extended, offering the amulet to the pirate without another word.

Hook's mouth twisted into a dark grin. "I'm not sure you understand what's happened," the pirate explained. He leaned forward like someone ready to share a secret. "I don't need you to *give* me anything, dear."

With a hand on Hope's shoulder, Hook thrust his sword through her stomach.

"No!"

Douglas lunged forward, but Hook's men buried the tips of their swords into his throat so any further movement would be suicide.

Hook watched with fascination as Hope slowly came to realize just what had happened. When he removed his sword, her lungs expelled air in a long wheeze.

It was the sound of someone's life being wrenched from their body.

Still sporting a menacing smile, Hook sheathed his sword then took the amulet from Hope's trembling hand. "If you don't mind..."

Helpless, Douglas watched, eyes swimming in tears as Hope stumbled about. She nearly fell over the balcony's edge before she was finally able to right herself. She turned, one hand on the rail, the other clutching her stomach's bloody wound. She looked to Douglas. A million silent thoughts passed between them in an instant, but one stood out above the rest...

She wanted him to get ready.

The thought was barely present in Douglas's mind when Hope threw herself forward and wrapped both hands around Hook's throat. The pirate had little trouble breaking away from her grip. Then, fueled by rage—

Hook shoved Hope over the balcony's rail.

Even his men were stunned by the abrupt and heinous move. Each stood frozen, mouths agape. And that was all the distraction Douglas needed.

In her last moments, Hope had given him his only chance at escape.

Douglas forced the swords away from his throat and scooped up his fallen pistol from the floor. One of the Queen's men thrust a spear at him. Douglas dropped to his knees and let it pass overhead.

Then, ignoring everyone else, Douglas leveled

his aim at Hook and fired. The bullet caught him in the shoulder and spun the pirate around like a top. Douglas was just about to fire his final bullet when he saw Hook's men closing on him. He quickly checked the door to see the Queen's remaining guard had blocked the exit. That left just one way off the balcony.

Douglas started for the ledge.

Hook's men swiped at Douglas with their swords, but none were able to connect. Instead, Douglas left them in a stupor, too shocked to take action as they watched him leap from the balcony, following behind his fallen friend, content to take his chances with the water that waited more than a hundred feet below.

CHAPTER 25

HOOK FOUND THE Queen looming over him.

"That may be the stupidest thing I've ever seen," she explained.

"I agree," Hook said. "The way he just threw himself off the balcony..."

"I was talking about *you*."

Hook staggered to his feet. His wound would slow him down, but it was clear the pirate had no intention of leaving the battle now that it had begun.

Smee and the other men stood near the balcony's ledge, all of them leaning over the rail for a chance to see what had become of Douglas. Unfortunately, morning mist had blanketed much of the moat, concealing the water below.

"We can't see him capt'n," Smee explained. "You think he made it?"

"Let's not leave it to chance. Take a few men to recover the body."

"Which one?"

"I want you to see if he survived," Hook growled.

"Oh! Right, right."

Smee led the rest of Hook's men out the door. The Queen motioned for her remaining guard to aide them in their search.

When they were gone, the Queen waited for the pirate to explain himself.

"This is what we discussed, your Highness."

"I didn't know you were going to do something like *that*."

"Now you do..."

The Queen wanted a better response than that.

"He was never going to make a deal with us," Hook explained. "The people in his world have no interest in letting us roam around doing as we see fit. They prefer to keep us in a box where we're expected to do their bidding and entertain."

"And now?" the Queen asked.

Hook took in their surroundings, looking down at the trail of blood that led to the balcony's ledge. He saw the bullet had opened two wounds in his shoulder: one where the bullet had entered, another on its way out. He gently touched the entry wound then tasted the blood it left on his fingertip. Strangely, this brought a smile to the pirate's face.

"Captain? What happens now?"

"I'm not sure I have an answer for that," Hook said.

"Excuse me?"

"Life's as it should be, Highness. Anything can happen. Anything at all."

❖ ❖ ❖

Douglas broke through the water's surface and gasped for air. Even with his head above water,

Douglas struggled to breathe. In fact, his body was so racked with pain, for a moment he wasn't sure he had survived at all.

Eventually collecting himself, Douglas was about to swim for the shoreline when he saw Hope's body floating facedown in the water nearby.

Adrenaline surged through him.

He splashed through the water, collected her body, and started for the shore. Once there, Douglas dragged Hope onto the muddy bank of the castle's moat then pulled her head into his lap. He gently moved wet strands of hair away from her face. He didn't even notice that he was now gently rocking as he cradled her lifeless body. He might have stayed like that forever if not for the sound of approaching voices...

"How we supposed to find these bodies if they sinked?" someone asked.

"Don't be a dolt," Smee answered. "Haven't you heard of the dead man's float? Once this bloody mist breaks, finding these two will be a cinch."

Douglas pushed to his feet. The rugged voices seemed to be filtering down to him from the castle's drawbridge across the way. If so, he had a head start of several minutes, plenty of time to make his escape...

Not that he felt inclined to take advantage.

Moving quickly now, Douglas concealed Hope's body behind some brush. Then he checked the cylinder of his revolver to learn only one bullet remained.

"The captain's feelin mighty bloody of late," someone slurred.

"Ain't he!"

"I've never seen him like this... not even with Pan!"

Four dark silhouettes appeared in the mist just ahead of Douglas. He readied his pistol, ready to fire upon the first pirate who dared step into view. But then something moved in the trees directly behind him. Douglas wheeled about, gun trained on the unexpected movement. Someone was closing in on him from the opposite direction as well. He was surrounded.

Head on a swivel, Douglas moved his attention back-and-forth between the pirates in the mist and the unseen strangers in the brush. Finally deciding those behind him presented an immediate risk, he leveled his weapon at the tree line, the gun an extension of his anger and hate as he pulled its hammer back. His finger hovered over the trigger. Ready. Waiting. So prepared to shoot that he nearly pulled the trigger when Wesley and The Librarian stepped into view.

The old man gasped. "Douglas?"

Douglas should have been relieved. He knew The Librarian would never harm him. And yet, Douglas couldn't shake a desire to fire anyway. A darkness existed within him that thought the last bullet in his gun was destined for the old man; that the universe had put The Librarian in his path for a reason.

Douglas stepped forward so the barrel of his gun was inches from the old man's face. His finger remained on the trigger: ready to give in to his anger and rage, ready to put an end to their epic rivalry once and for all.

"She didn't deserve this," Douglas said, his voice little more than a waver.

"Neither did you," The Librarian said softly.

Douglas let his arm drop just as his legs gave out from under him. He would have collapsed into the dirt if the old man had not stepped forward to catch him, wrapping both arms around his former apprentice just as he began to sob.

CHAPTER 26

RANDY LET TAY sleep. There was no point waking her. They'd already exhausted every scenario that might lead to escape. None had worked. They were stuck in the Queen's dungeon until she sent someone to let them out. The way things were going outside, Randy thought that might be sooner than later.

Wonderland's residents were starting to gather in the castle's courtyard. The sun was high, but it seemed many wanted to arrive well before sundown to ensure they got good seats. Apparently some in Wonderland were as excited to see blood spilled as the Queen.

Standing at the window, Randy shifted his gaze to the forest that bordered the courtyard. While he was nervous about his own predicament, he'd spent most of the last hour wondering where his dad might be. Was he still out there in search of Randy and Tay; or had he made his way back to the castle? Did he know what was about to happen? If so, would he try to save Randy and Tay?

The question had barely entered his mind when Randy had a vision of his father appearing from the tree line to storm the castle. The thought put a smile on his face, but those warm feelings didn't last. The Queen's men were already set to guard the caste: every playing-card in the pack along with her armored guards.

Maybe it was best that his father and the others just stayed away.

Anyone who tried to stop the executions wouldn't stand much of a chance.

❖ ❖ ❖

Frozen by grief, Douglas was reluctant to leave his friend behind. Luckily, The Librarian was eventually able to console him and pull Douglas away from Hope's carefully hidden body. Together with Wes, they fled into the woods just in time to evade Hook's men.

Wesley couldn't help but think that their situation had gotten worse. Even if Douglas was willing to put his selfish plans aside, he was certain Douglas would come unglued when he learned Wesley and the old man had allowed Randy to give himself up.

After hurrying to safety, the trio finally stopped to rest. When they did, Douglas explained just what Hook had done. Then The Librarian was forced to tell his former apprentice that Hook and the Queen had captured his son.

Douglas didn't blow up the way Wes thought he might. Instead, he walked away from them to be alone with his thoughts. He kept to himself for nearly an hour, pacing back-and-forth with his eyes on the ground.

Eventually, Wesley thought they'd stewed in silence long enough. "How long are we going to just sit around like this?" he whispered to The Librarian. "We've only got a few hours, and we haven't even talked about what we're going to do."

The old man left Wesley to join Douglas near the ridge where he was standing. At first, Douglas did little to acknowledge the old man's presence, and The Librarian wasn't sure how to begin.

"My boy thinks I want revenge," Douglas finally said. "Can you believe that?"

The old man shook his head. "I see it differently. The boy I met all those years ago didn't have an ounce of hate in his heart. You may have strayed from the path, but most of us have at some point. Believe me, you aren't the first."

"That's a whole lot of words just to say you agree with him."

The Librarian opened his mouth to refute this, but Douglas wouldn't let him.

"You know what's funny: I told myself I was doing this because my childhood was stolen from me. I almost did the exact same thing to my son." Douglas shook his head, his gaze moving to his feet. "I've *already* done it to him."

The Librarian laid a hand on Douglas's shoulder. "Our story is far from over."

"Let's hope you're right."

Both men made their way back to where Wesley sat perched on a large boulder. Douglas removed his amulet and held it out for Wesley to take.

"I assume you know how to use one of these."

Wesley rose to his feet. "I do, but—"

Douglas cut him off. "I don't want anyone else to get hurt because of me, kid."

"I'm not going anywhere."

"Kid…"

"Stop calling me that. After everything that's happened, you're lucky we're trusting you at all. Who goes and who stays isn't your call to make."

Douglas looked to The Librarian beside him for help.

"I think we need all the help we can get," the old man explained.

"Can he take care of himself?"

"If he ever gets out of his own way."

Wesley furrowed his brow. He wasn't sure that was meant to be reassuring.

"Okay," Douglas began, "then it's the three of us."

"You said the children are to be executed this evening. When they're brought into the courtyard at sundown, we'll be waiting."

Douglas shook his head. "No. No way. That's cutting it too close."

"I agree it's too close for comfort, but anything earlier than that would require more time to plan and more manpower than the three of us can give. Imagine it: we'd have to infiltrate the castle, find the children, break them free, and escape without being seen by the Queen's men. It's an impossible task."

"Then there's no room for error. And we still have to deal with the guards."

Wesley finally found it was time for him to speak up. "Why can't we just distract them? That's what they would do in the movies, right? Create a big enough distraction so we can save them while everyone is looking the other way."

"Okay," Douglas said. "What are we talking about?"

"Maybe we can set the castle on fire," Wesley said.

"It's made of stone. I don't think that'll work."

All three stood in silence for a long moment.

"What if we lured the Jabberwock out of hiding?" Wesley asked sheepishly.

Douglas sighed. "Be realistic, kid. We don't know where the Jabberwock is.

The Librarian answered for Wesley. "We do, actually. It's sleeping in a cave in the mountains not far from here."

Suddenly excited, Wes began to pace. "Don't you see? When we were trapped in the caves you said it might be for a reason. Maybe this is it.

"How would we lure it out in the first place?" Douglas asked.

"He's protecting this giant mountain of treasure. So... we steal it."

Neither of the men seemed to think this was a good idea.

"It'll work," Wesley insisted.

"It might," The Librarian said.

Douglas shook his head. "I still don't like it."

"Why not?"

"Even if everything else works out perfectly, the whole thing hinges on the Jabberwock following us down the mountain. There's no way we can guarantee that happens."

Wesley's shoulders slumped forward. Douglas was right. They couldn't bet everything on the Jabberwock actually doing what they wanted it to do. With no room for error, they had to make sure their plan left nothing to chance.

The moment dragged, each of them lost in his own thoughts. Then Wesley was struck by an idea so crazy, it just might work.

"What if we *can* guarantee the Jabberwock follows us into the courtyard?"

CHAPTER 27

RANDY WAS CURLED up in a spot beside Taylor where he'd fallen asleep. Unfortunately, he wasn't there long before one of the Queen's guards appeared outside the dungeon cells and rattled his large ring of keys to awaken the prisoners.

"Rise and shine, conspirators."

The gryphon stirred in its cell, momentarily forgetting it didn't have room to stretch its wings. Nearby, the Duchess rose into a seated position, sadness in her deeply-set eyes when she saw her surroundings remained unchanged.

The guard seemed to delight in their despair. A black grin darkened his face as he turned to check on the others, but it immediately dropped into a frown when he saw the Hatter and the Hare were still sound asleep... and snoring.

"Did you hear what I said?" he sneered. "On your feet!"

The guard strummed his keys across the prison bars. The Hatter popped to his feet with a start. Beside him, the Hare leapt several feet into the air.

"Oh my!" the Hatter explained. "Are we late for tea?"

The Hare fumbled about to find his cup then held it out in a trembling hand.

"Sure," the guard smirked. "That's just where we're going. The two of you are set to have tea with the Queen. We just have one stop to make first."

Showing great interest, the Hatter stepped forward. "What kind of stop?"

"You've got an appointment with the executioner."

The Hatter pulled back from the cell door and shrank into the shadows.

Content to see he'd filled their cups with fear, the guard turned to check on Randy and Tay. "As for you two…" He raised his hand to show a tangle of heavy handcuffs and shackles hanging from his closed fist. "I'm here to help you get ready for the ball."

◆ ◆ ◆

Wesley needed a head start if he was going to get into position.

Meanwhile, after seeing the boy off, Douglas and The Librarian stationed themselves behind a series of large boulders. Positioned near a dirt road, they were able to watch as people streamed into town to witness the executions.

It was a strange sight for both to see. The people carried themselves with a carefree excitement, as if they were off to see a concert or play. Many had their children in tow. Others had packed wagons like they were prepared to make a day of it. It was these people Douglas and the old man were most interested in.

"It's going to be tough stealing a wagon with so many people around," Douglas explained. "What are we going to do about witnesses?"

"The crowd will thin out as we get closer to sundown," The Librarian said. "We'll wait until this procession is down to a mere trickle before we act."

Douglas lifted his attention to the setting sun. "I'm not sure we have time to wait. Maybe we should just take the next wagon that comes along and be done with it. If we have to knock out of a few witness, so be it. Serves them right getting this amped up to see a bunch of people killed anyway."

The old man didn't like the edge in Douglas's voice. It reminded him all too well of the half-dozen altercations he'd had with the man over the years, including the one that had left him with a nasty burn on his arm that was just starting to heal. Good lord, that moment in his study felt like a lifetime ago given everything that had happened. In reality, it had only been a matter of days.

"It's important that we're patient," The Librarian said. "It's when people cut corners that mistakes are made. And I'll agree with you on one thing: if this is to work like the boy hopes, there's no room for error."

Douglas nodded in agreement. Then: "The kid is special, isn't he?"

"It's more than that. I think he could become an Author."

Douglas arched both eyebrows in surprise.

"I wouldn't read too much into that," the old man explained. "It's been so long since the Muse touched anyone with his magic. Still, there was a moment in Oz... with Dorothy... I thought he was one of the Authors already."

The possibility stirred something in Douglas. He was lost in his thoughts for a long moment, standing quietly beside The Librarian as he watched another group of people walk by. "There's something I need to tell you," Douglas explained. "When this whole started I made it sound as if one of the Elders was helping me. That isn't entirely true..."

"I don't understand. Where would you have gotten an amulet?"

Douglas frowned, shame dimming his face. "It was made for me..."

CHAPTER 28

WESLEY DID HIS best to blend in with those traveling the dirt road into town. He'd stolen a cloak that allowed him to hide his face beneath a dark hood, but he found it hard to keep his head down given all the activity unfolding outside the Queen's castle.

One might think the kingdom was preparing for a grand celebration. Half-a-dozen clowns wandered the crowd, each performing for any children that happened along. A pair of fire-breathing wolves stood on tall platforms near the castle's drawbridge, both blowing long streams of flame after filling their mouths with a strange liquid kept in wooden jugs. Court jesters juggled live geese. There was even a sword-swallowing giraffe being fed sharp blades by a peculiar looking pig in a suit and top hat. It was Wonderland's version of a carnival, an incredible sight to behold...

And the whole thing made Wesley sick.

It was bad enough to know this many people had left home to watch people die – to see they were treating the event like a party made it all the worse.

Wes slowly made his way forward where he hoped to be swallowed up by the crowd. He may have been disgusted by their presence, but he knew the mob of onlookers would make it easier for him to go unnoticed by the Queen's men. He pulled the hood down over his head and started through the gate, careful to avert his eyes as he walked past a pair of playing-card soldiers standing at attention on either side of the entrance. One of the men was barking orders to the crowd. "No blades. No bows. Leave your weapons here."

Two men just ahead of Wesley dropped unsheathed knives and added them to a pile of weapons already collected. For a brief moment, Wesley worried one of the soldiers would ask him to drop his staff before allowing him to pass – but neither did.

Once safely through the gate, Wes saw the Queen and King were sitting together in risers near the courtyard. An unusual group of talking animals sat crowded around them: birds, bears, chickens, and apes. There were even a few animals Wesley didn't recognize: strange, hybrid beasts unique to Wonderland.

He worked his way through the crowd toward the platform at the opposite end of the field. Apparently Wesley had made it just in time. He was only halfway through the crowd when the White Rabbit appeared in the bleachers with a trumpet.

"Here ye, here ye!" the Rabbit yelled. "We are gathered here today in honor of the true royalty, a woman we each hold in the highest regard, the highest of the highnesses, our very own: Queen of Hearts."

The crowd swelled with applause. The Queen waved to show her approval.

"We're so lucky to have her," the Rabbit said. "Would you agree?"

Cheers erupted from the courtyard...

"Long live the Queen of Hearts!" a baker screamed.

"May her rule never end!" a grey wolf howled.

Then, as if they'd rehearsed it a thousand times, everyone in the crowd repeated the baker's sentiment in unison. *"Long live the Queen!"*

"Yes, yes," the Rabbit responded. "You are loyal subjects. As you should be. But as I'm sure you've discovered, there are traitors in our midst: those who would take sides against the Queen of Hearts and all that her kingdom stands for." The Rabbit lifted his chin into the air. *"Bring out the Friends of Alice!"*

Everyone turned in unison. They watched as a large, wrought-iron gate creaked open to reveal a stone stairwell that disappeared into the castle's dungeon. Moments later, one of the Jokers stepped from the shadows. Many in the crowd gasped. A few children began to cry. For some, this was their first chance to see the horrific duo tasked with carrying out the Queen's bloodiest order. But Wesley had seen them before. Heck, he'd seen worse in Oz. He was unaffected by the Jokers' presence. Instead, Wes felt his stomach tighten when Taylor stepped from the darkness of the dungeon. Sight of her shackled feet and chained wrists helped Wesley understand just how high the stakes had become.

Several guards cleared a path through the crowd for the prisoners.

"Get back there! Make way."

Most in the crowd did as they were told. But it wasn't long before the onlookers were pushing forward, everyone desperate to get a good look at the captives. And for some, a look wasn't enough...

"You're getting what you deserve!" a woman yelled.

"The chopping block's too good for you!" a walrus shouted.

Some booed. Others threw rocks.

The prisoners had to duck for cover, shielding themselves as best they could while making their way up the staircase and onto the executioner's platform.

It took everything Wesley had to keep quiet. Revealing himself would destroy any chance they had at escape.

He'd have to stand back and watch as the people of Wonderland abused her.

❖ ❖ ❖

Douglas dragged his victim through the dirt, making sure to gently lower the unconscious giant to the ground where he and The Librarian had been hiding just a few moments ago.

In truth, Douglas felt bad for the guy. He'd been

in the wrong place at the wrong time: riding his wagon into town when he happened upon a pair of men in need of help. How was he to know Douglas was going to club him over the head?

With the stranger tucked away, Douglas hurried back to find The Librarian inspecting the horse-drawn wagon they'd just stolen.

"Anyone see?" he asked.

"I'm more concerned with the condition of this wagon."

The Librarian gestured to the rickety vehicle, and Douglas moved to check it out himself. Sure enough, its wood was badly weathered. Many of its boards were loose. Its wheels were misshapen and connected by axles that looked like they might snap at any moment. When he climbed into the wagon for a closer look, the entire thing seemed to buckle and whine beneath his weight. Even the horse looked back with concern.

Douglas hopped down. "It's all we've got," he said. "As long as it makes it down the hill we're good."

"You're sure you can get it there?"

"Are you kidding? My job's easy compared to yours..."

Douglas forced a smile, but The Librarian sensed a hint of worry in his voice. Not that the old man blamed him. His son's life was on the line, and with everything now in place, their success rested squarely on the old man's shoulders – and The Librarian wasn't the man he used to be.

❖ ❖ ❖

Back in the courtyard, the prisoners had finally made it through the crowd and onto the executioner's platform. Once there, the Jokers shoved them to their knees. The Hatter was thrown forward with such force that his hat scooted from his head and fell to the ground below.

"I must say," the Hatter began, "if I'm to lose my head I would very much like to know I was wearing one of my finest hats. Is there any chance you'll shuffle down to retrieve it, sir?"

The Joker looked down on the Hatter with dead eyes then moved on.

"I suppose that's a no..."

Beside the Hatter, Randy scanned the crowd. There was no sign of Wesley or the old man. Taylor was coming to the same realization.

The thought they might be on their own barely had time to take hold before the White Rabbit blew his trumpet and the crowd fell silent once more.

"Each of the despicable creatures before you has failed to put the Queen's kingdom first as law dictates. Having been found guilty by a jury of their peers, we've brought them before you today so that their sentences may be carried out."

One of the Jokers started toward a small table near the chopping block. A woven blanket was stretched across its surface. When he reached the table, the Joker removed the blanket to reveal several impossibly sharp instruments: including a mammoth executioner's axe.

When the Joker reached for the axe, Randy sprung to his feet.

"Wait a minute! Aren't we supposed to get some last words?"

"Prisoners can say all they want *after* their sentence is carried out," the Rabbit explained.

"After? Really? Tell me: is everyone in those bleachers stupid or is it just me?"

The crowd gasped.

The White Rabbit shook his head and made a clicking sound to signal his disapproval. "I would watch your step, young man."

"Why? Are you going to cut my head off again?" Randy looked into the crowd. "We're up here because we're different, because the Queen thinks we were friends with someone she doesn't like. Guess what: she doesn't like anyone! Besides, look round: we're all different, right? That's what makes Wonderland so great. But what happens when you're the wrong kind of different? How long will it be before the Queen's is calling for your head because she doesn't like the way you look or the way you dress or the way you think? How long before people are calling you guilty without hearing your side?"

Still in hiding, Wesley couldn't believe it.

Randy Stanford was standing up for the little guy.

Looking about, Wes waited for the crowd's reaction. Many scrunched their brows in confusion. Others looked about to see how their neighbors might react. For a moment, Wes thought Randy had changed some minds.

Then the laughter came.

It started with a quiet snort from a chubby pig in the front row with his family, but it wasn't long before the infectious laughter had washed over the entire crowd.

"I've heard enough," the Queen shouted. "Off with their heads!"

One of the Jokers started toward the Hatter. He was about to yank him to his feet when the Queen called out to him from the stands.

"Leave the Hatter for now. Start with the one the boy loves so much..."

Randy and Tay looked to one another in horror.

"Start with the girl."

◆ ◆ ◆

Wesley watched with a growing sense of dread as the Jokers yanked Taylor to her feet and dragged her toward the chopping block. Randy tried to intervene, but he was quickly restrained by a pair of armored guards.

Wes swung around in a panic, eyes moving to the gate.

Douglas and the old man were nowhere in sight.

And there was no time to spare.

The Joker forced Tay to her knees. He shoved

her forward so her face was pressed down on the executioner's block. Behind her, Randy kicked at the air in an effort to break free from the soldiers' grip.

The crowd roared.

"How can you cheer?" Randy screamed. *"What is wrong with you people?"*

His questions fell on deaf ears. The crowd of onlookers was now nothing more than a mob now: a living, breathing organism, united by a thirst for blood.

"Someone, do something!"

Wesley pulled the staff from beneath his cloak and pushed his way to the front of the crowd. Those in the mob were so entranced that they didn't even notice. It was only when Wesley let his cloak drop to the ground that one of the Queen's guards saw him, realizing Wes wasn't watching with a vacant stare or droning on in the chorus of hate with everyone else.

"Wait," the guard said. "You there! Stop!"

Ignoring the order, Wesley quickened his pace.

The guard gestured for two of his men to step in and stop him.

"That boy there! Grab him!"

One of the Jokers took the axe from the table as two of the Queen's men pursued Wesley through the crowd.

One of the guards blindsided Wes and grabbed for his arm. Wes spun away, letting his staff lead the way until it cracked the stranger across his chin.

When his attacker went down, Wes swung around without looking and caught the second guard in the face as well.

This was finally enough to get the attention of some in the mob.

Even those in the royal box were beginning to take notice of the commotion.

And yet, the Jokers went about the grisly business at hand...

Now standing over Tay, the executioner lowered his axe so it kissed the back of her neck. She recoiled from the touch of cold metal. Then the Joker raised his weapon into the air.

"No! No! No!" Still thirty feet away, Wesley wasn't going to make it in time.

Tay closed her eyes. The executioner started down with the axe.

"Taylor!"

With the Joker's blade descending, Wesley planted his feet and pushed the staff forward. As the staff arced through the air, its stone came alive with light. Not that Wesley noticed. He wasn't watching. Instinct had told him to close his eyes. He wasn't even sure what he was doing until it happened – until that light shot out from his staff and grabbed hold of the Joker's axe.

The crowd gasped. The guards froze. When Wes finally had the courage to open his eyes, he couldn't believe it himself.

On the platform, Taylor looked about in confusion.

Then her gaze landed on her friend.

"Wes?"

The two locked eyes. Happy tears streaked her cheeks.

She was finally able to breath again.

"*Guards!*" the Queen screamed.

Wesley pulled back on the staff. The stone's energy yanked the axe free of the executioner's hands and sent it flying end-over-end into the crowd.

Randy saw the Queen's army descending on Wesley. "*Bates! Behind you!*"

Wes wheeled around to find the King had sent the entire pack onto the field.

"*Don't let him get away,*" he ordered. "*I want that boy caught!*"

"*No!*" the Queen screamed. "*Execute him!*"

The crowd made room so the soldiers could easily surround Wes.

But even with superior numbers, they were reluctant to engage.

The Queen rose to her feet. "*What are you waiting for? Take him!*"

The soldiers inched forward. Wes lifted his staff, but he wasn't exactly sure what he was going to do. It had taken everything he had to disarm the Joker, and he wasn't even sure how he'd done that.

The circle tightened until the entire pack of playing-card men was within striking distance. They were just about to attack when Wesley heard something approaching from outside the castle gate...

Confusion washed over the crowd as they turned to see what was causing this new commotion. Of course, Wesley recognized what was happening almost immediately. After all, they were listening to the gallop of a racing horse; the bump-and-grind of a wooden wagon bouncing across rough terrain.

"Look out!" someone screamed.

Douglas guided the stolen wagon onto the playing field at full speed. Its back end had caught fire so it left a trail of orange flame smoking in its wake.

Making matters worse, the wagon was heading straight for the grandstands.

"Move!" Douglas yelled. *"Out of the way!"*

The onlookers darted for cover. The horse was about to pull away so it didn't run headfirst into the grandstands. Douglas cut it free to ensure the wagon continued on its current path... straight for the King and Queen.

The Queen's eyes widened. "What? No. Stop. Stop I say!"

Douglas leapt from the wagon.

In the stands, the King pushed several of his subjects out of the way so he and the Queen could escape. Some jumped over the side. Squawking in fear, a pair of tuxedoed birds took to the air. The royal couple barely escaped themselves, falling to the ground in a heap just as the wagon smashed into the risers and set them ablaze.

Wesley hurried over as Douglas got to his feet. "You okay?"

Douglas answered with a harried nod.

"I don't understand," Wesley began, "where's—"

"The Jabberwock!"

All eyes turned upward just in time to see the dragon drop down from the heavens above. The winged beast landed with a heavy thud, the earth quaking as it spit an angry stream of blue fire into the sky.

The crowd's fear turned to panic in an instant. Covered in green scales, the Jabberwock towered forty feet above them. It looked like a young child's strange drawing come to life. It's buck-toothed face was framed in long whiskers. Antenna sprouted from between the Jabberwock's bulging eyes. The dragon stood on two feet, and its claws were so large Wes thought the Jabberwock could easily crush a car between them.

The Queen's soldiers turned their gaze to the attacking dragon. The Jokers leapt from the platform and hurried over. Both were armed and ready to fight the beast as the crowd scattered, running for their lives.

Douglas turned to Wes beside him. "Alright, kid. Go get 'em!"

Wesley sprinted toward the executioner's platform. He pressed through the crowd and did his best to avoid the Queen's soldiers, but even those who saw him paid Wesley little mind. They had more pressing concerns...

The Jabberwock was already working to stir up trouble. It had whipped its long tail down to block those trying to escape and was now batting soldiers away with its mammoth claws before any of them could get close enough to attack.

Wesley stomped up the steps onto the platform.

Hands bound behind her back, Tay pushed to her feet.

"Wesley..."

"Hey."

"Hey?" Taylor exclaimed. "That's all you can think to say? Hey!"

Wesley shrugged as Randy and the other prisoners formed a circle around him. Randy gestured to Wesley's staff. "Can you use that thing to unlock us?"

"We're about to find out."

Wes looked down into the chaos of the courtyard. The mob had morphed into a full on stampede. People screamed. Children shrieked in terror. Those frozen in place risked being trampled to death as Wonderland's residents fled into the woods with little regard for anyone around them. Meanwhile, both Jokers had joined the Queen's soldiers to aid in the battle against the Jabberwock.

"We've got to hurry," Wesley explained. "They may be stupid, but the Queen's men won't be fooled for very long."

"What do you mean?" Randy asked.

"That's not the real Jabberwock."

CHAPTER 29

HOOK AND HIS men watched from the sidelines as the battle progressed.

Archers rushed to find high ground so they could rain arrows down on the beast. Infantry men tried to close on the monster with their swords and spears, but the Jabberwock just swatted them away with ease.

Strangely, the soldiers who got close enough to attack saw their weapons had little impact on the Jabberwock. Thrown spears seemed to bounce off the dragon's scaly skin. Thrusting swords never drew blood. Even the Jokers' lethal hats were of little use. It wasn't that the Jabberwock was over-powering the Queen's army. It was like the dragon was impervious to their attacks, as if it couldn't be hurt at all.

"Capt'n, I think we're wise to sit this one out," Smee said. "There ain't no beatin that awful thing. Should I tell the men it's time to leave?"

"Not yet, Smee."

Hook scanned the crowd for anything out of place. Everything was as he expected given the circumstance. People were running for their lives.

Then his eyes fell on Douglas Stanford.

He was the man who'd led the Jabberwock onto

the field...

And he didn't seem to be scared at all.

"What is going on?" Hook muttered beneath his breath.

What happened next did little to answer the captain's question.

The Jabberwock disappeared.

It happened in a fraction of a second, really. The dragon blinked out of existence then reappeared in a flash. Only a few in the crowd noticed at all, and those who did weren't even sure what they'd seen.

But Hook saw it for what it was: proof something was amiss.

"What is going on?" he repeated.

The dragon brought its tail down on the grandstands so they exploded in a cloud of splinters, but something about the beast was definitely off. As the fight wore on, the monster's coloring dimmed until it appeared almost trans-lucent, nothing more than a shadow of the beast that had landed in the field.

Nearby, a trio of archers had finally made their way to high ground. Once there, the marksmen let their arrows fly. And their aim was perfect.

But the arrows passed through the Jabberwock like it wasn't even there.

"Are you thinkin we should help, capt'n?"

Hook watched with fascination as the Jabber-wock swung its taloned hand at a group of charging soldiers. This time the move didn't send the soldiers flying as it had before. In fact—

The dragon's hand passed *through* the soldiers without disturbing them at all.

"Capt'n?"

Finally, as the soldiers closed in, the Jabberwock threw back its head and shot a ribbon of blue flame at the platoon of playing-card men. It hit the paper soldiers head-on and should have ignited them on contact – but it didn't.

The flame was as weak and useless as the Jabberwock had become.

Hook moved his attention to the executioner's platform where Wesley was working to free the prisoners.

"It's a trick!"

"What's that?" Smee asked.

Before Hook could answer the Jabberwock disappeared entirely.

The Queen's men looked about in stunned disbelief. Somehow, the dragon's disappearance was almost as chilling as the monster itself.

But as they took in the destruction, their confusion quickly morphed to anger, all of it directed at the man who had lured the Jabberwock through the gate.

Douglas grabbed a discarded spear from the ground. The Jabberwock had thinned the Queen's army, but Douglas was still in for an impossible fight.

Luckily, he wasn't alone long.

Just as the soldiers were about to make their move, a cloaked figure appeared from inside the wagon and took a defensive position beside Douglas. If it wasn't for the staff in his hand, most would assume the old man looked out of place on a battle field. With his tailored vest and wire spectacles, he looked like the kind of man who spent most of his time in a library.

◆ ◆ ◆

Wesley unlocked the gryphon then watched as it took to the sky and flew away.

Randy scoffed. "Dude didn't even say thanks."

Free himself, the Hatter was about to retrieve his fallen hat when he saw the Jokers were now racing over to stop them, one of them hurrying toward each of the staircases on either side of the wooden platform.

"Oh my!" the Duchess exclaimed. "We're too late! We're trapped!"

"It's fine," Wesley said. "We'll hold them off so you can escape."

"We can stay to help," the Hatter explained.

"No. It's too important you live to fight another day."

The Hatter bowed his head then he and the Hare hurried down the stairs. Strangely, the Jokers let them pass without much fuss. It seemed the bony assassins were far more interested in the kids who had started this mess.

Wes checked on Douglas and The Librarian. The two adults stood back-to-back as they battled the

Queen's men. They seemed to be winning, but Wes noticed The Librarian was already tiring. It wouldn't be long before Douglas would be left to fight on his own.

"They're coming," Taylor whispered.

The Jokers were now climbing the stairs and would soon be closing in on them from either side. Wes raised his staff as Randy and Tay helped the Duchess down from the platform.

"You can fight them off, right?" Randy asked nervously.

"Not like this," Wesley explained.

"What about that thing you just did to save Tay?"

"I have no idea how that happened..."

The Jokers stepped onto the platform, ready to close on the children from both sides. The first had recovered his axe and was ready to strike. The other was twirling his razor-brimmed top hat between his fingers.

Click-clack.

Clack! Clack! Clack!

The kids bunched together in a tight circle.

"You do have a plan, right?" Taylor asked.

"As a matter of fact, I do."

Wesley pulled a wilted mushroom from his pocket.

"Stand back," Wesley explained.

Randy and Tay came together a few steps behind Wes as he took a bite from the magic mushroom. Both watched with anticipation as—

Nothing happened.

Just a few feet away, one of the Jokers poked at them with the handle of his axe. The other swiped at Wes with the brim of his hat. Both seemed to miss on purpose, as if killing the children wouldn't be enough.

Apparently, they wanted to watch the kids give up on life before taking it.

"Okay," Randy smirked. "Now will you try to do something with your staff?"

Before Wesley could answer, the first Joker threw his hat at Wes. With little space between them, all Wesley could do was drop and hope for the best. The spinning hat whistled by his head, so close it ruffled his hair.

"Wesley!" Taylor shouted. "Look out!"

On his back, Wesley looked up just in time to see the second Joker's axe coming down on him. Helpless from his position, Wes closed his eyes and ducked for cover. He threw both hands into the air, hoping they might slow the Joker's blade enough that he was able to survive the executioner's strike.

But just as before, the blow never landed. Wes opened his eyes, stealing a quick glance to see what had happened. Somehow he'd caught the axe's blade between his palms—

Palms *four times* their normal size.

Randy and Tay watched as Wesley's metamorphosis moved across his body in a wave. His arms stretched like saltwater taffy, looking impossibly thin until muscle expanded to match the length. His shoulder came next. They blew up so his torso looked like an inverted triangle: big, broad shoulders tampering off to a point at Wesley's boyish waist. Of course, his waist wasn't tiny long. It swelled along with his legs, the two appendages thrusting Wesley's body into the air like a pair of magic beanstalks. Finally, his head caught up, quadrupling in size as he reached his full height of nearly thirty feet.

There was a new giant looming in the Queen's courtyard.

His name was Wesley Bates.

Douglas looked to The Librarian beside him. "Where did you find this kid?"

"He found me," the old man grinned. "The same as you."

Douglas couldn't share the old man's smile. The Librarian looked out on his feet, like he might collapse at any moment. He wasn't going to last much longer.

Back on the platform, Wes tossed the axe aside then shifted his attention to the Jokers at his feet. While the dark assassins had taken a few steps back, both were ready to reengage. They clenched their bony jaws and charged at Wes, their lethal hats leading the way.

Wesley lumbered a bit, the platform trembling beneath his giant sneakers as he got used to his new size. He got his balance just in time to bat the hats out of the sky. Then, Wesley reeled back his foot and let it fly...

For a kid who was often picked last for kickball,

Wesley had no problem connecting with both Jokers. He kicked the playing-card men with such force that they soared through the air until they were out of sight.

Some claim neither ever came down.

Seeing the assassins dispatched so easily enraged the King of Clubs beyond reason. *"Kill the outsiders! Kill them all!"*

Wesley looked over to see the Queen's soldiers were no longer taking turns in their attack on Douglas and The Librarian. They were swarming the pair in one last-ditch effort to gain the upper hand.

Wes dropped to one knee beside his friends. He waited for Randy's permission then gently lifted him off the ground with a single hand. When he had Randy secure, Wesley looked over at Taylor.

"Who's the big man on campus now?"

Taylor blushed, so smitten she had to look away. Wesley didn't notice. His eyes were fixed on the armored guards approaching as he wrapped his hand around Tay.

"Let's go home," Wesley said.

"Definitely," Taylor added.

Wesley rose to his feet and jumped down from the platform. The earth trembled beneath, announcing his arrival onto the battlefield.

Wes wasn't able to dispense with the approaching soldiers as easily as he'd been able to dismiss the Jokers. There were just too many. A few landed blows, opening thin cuts on each of Wesley's legs just below the knees. But Wes never let this slow him down. Whenever one of the Queen's men was within range, he let his feet do the talking...

He kicked men into the woods. He flattened others beneath his shoe. One he grabbed between two fingers and flung over the castle like a paper airplane. In fact, he was so dominant that it wasn't long before those that remained turned to flee as everyone else already had.

Wesley crossed the field in three giant strides. He knelt to the dirt when he reached Douglas and The Librarian. "You guys need a lift?"

"Oh my god!" Taylor exclaimed. "You aren't that funny."

"I don't know," Wesley said. "It's kinda funny."

Ignoring the banter, Douglas helped The Librarian climb onto Wesley's back. It was only then that Wesley noticed just how weak the old man had become.

"Is he okay?" Wesley asked.

"I'm fine," The Librarian croaked. "Just... head that way."

The old man's condition filled Wes with concern, but he quickly pushed the worry aside and did as he was told, rising to his feet and starting toward a gap in trees that offered an easy escape.

Happy to have the chaotic battle behind them, no one saw Captain Hook and his men had blocked the Queen's soldiers from fleeing into the woods.

No one saw, and thus, no one knew to ask the ever-important question... why?

CHAPTER 30

WESLEY AND THE others quickly put distance between themselves and the Queen's castle. When they felt like they were far enough out, Wes helped everyone to the ground. He was careful when lowering The Librarian, gently placing him beneath a large shade tree in the meadow.

Once on solid ground, Douglas took charge, telling Taylor to stay with The Librarian while he and Randy went in search of a mushroom that would return Wesley to his regular size. Luckily, The Librarian was up-and-moving again when Douglas and his son finally returned.

"How are you feeling?" Douglas asked.

"Fair enough," The Librarian answered. "I don't recover as quickly as I once did, but I can't imagine anyone does at my age."

"I don't understand why using magic makes you tired like that," Randy said.

"The mind is a muscle like any other, young man. It can be strengthened. It can grow weak. Aren't you tired after doing your studies?"

"Randy doesn't study," Taylor said.

Randy smirked. "Where's Bates?"

Tay pointed to a nearby cavern, its entrance a web of shadows. "You can come out now."

Wesley appeared from within the cave. Framed in its entrance, Wes was hunched over so his chin rested on his knees. It was all he could do to prevent hitting his head on the overhang as he stepped into the open.

"Were you guys able to find anything?" Wesley asked.

Randy dropped a black mushroom into Wesley's extended hand. The large toadstool looked tiny in Wesley's massive palm.

"So what do we do now?" Taylor asked. "Are we going home?"

Sadness washed over Douglas. "What are things like in Astoria right now?"

"You don't want to know," the old man explained.

"We'll never be able to undo what I've done, will we?"

The Librarian didn't have an answer for that.

"What about *The Manuscript*?" Wesley asked.

The old man shook his head. "The Elders would never allow that."

"What are you talking about?" Taylor asked.

"*The Manuscript* is this book in the library that will give whoever has it control of the real world the way an author controls one of the storybook lands."

"You're kidding?!"

"It's out of the question," The Librarian said

sternly.

"But what's the point of having something like that if you aren't going to use it? Don't you think it's for a situation just like this?"

"I feel like I've had this conversation before," Douglas murmured.

"The truth is: *The Manuscript* is something of a myth. We believe it is buried beneath the library, but we don't know where. Even if we did, we aren't sure how to use it. Besides, who knows what could happen if magic like that fell into the wrong hands? It's better off hidden away where no one can get to it."

"I'm not sure we need it anyway," Douglas said. "Part of me thinks we're supposed to be here, that all of this is happening for a reason."

"How can you possibly say that?" Wesley asked.

"Think about it: the Queen was rounding up the Friends of Alice *before* we arrived. She was going to rule forever like that if we'd never shown up."

"What are you saying?" the old man asked.

"What if we're exactly where we're supposed to be? What if destiny guides us the way it guides these fairy-tale characters? What if there's a reason you were never able to send me back to my old life?"

These were all questions without answers.

"So what do we do?" Taylor asked.

"Hook wants to escape into the real world. We stop him before he has a chance."

The Librarian stroked the length of his beard. "Even if we were able, how would we return them to Neverland so the *Pan* story is restored?"

"I can convince him to go back," Douglas said. "I know I can."

Silence dropped over the group. No one else shared Douglas's confidence.

He leaned into The Librarian, ready to make one final plea. "Please. Just... give me a chance to fix this... even if you're sure I can't... let me try."

"Very well," The Librarian said.

The old man took up his staff and satchel like he was ready to go. The others prepared to leave with him. Wesley was just about to pop the mushroom into his mouth when Randy spoke up.

"Wait a minute!" he exclaimed. "I almost forgot."

"What is it, son?"

"We can't go back. Not yet." Randy shot a smile at Taylor. "There's something we have to do first."

CHAPTER 31

ADRIENNE AND JEZEBEL were beginning to worry. The knights had been keeping watch for Randy and Tay since early that morning, but the day had since come and gone.

As the moon began to move across the starry sky, both queens had to consider the children might not return. If they didn't, the other pieces in the set would be looking to them for leadership. Neither was excited by the prospect. Sure they often fought over control of their board, but this was the real world. Their decisions would carry real consequences and neither Adrienne nor Jezebel was ready to take the lead. Not like this...

One of the knights pulled on his horse's reins and rode over to the queens.

"It's them," he said excitedly. "The children have returned."

The announcement was enough to get all of the tired pieces to their feet. Each hurried to the edge of the garden, clambering for a look. A few pawns got stuck behind taller pieces, but they were still able to share in the excitement when the others confirmed what the knight had said.

The rooks applauded. The bishops thanked the heavens for answered prayers. Several pieces embraced their neighbor, relieved to know the long ordeal might be coming to an end. And in the end, they all watched with broad smiles as Randy and Taylor led a trio of new faces through the gate.

Adrienne smoothed her wooden dress when Taylor fell to one knee near the garden's edge. "We were beginning to think you two forgot about us," she said.

Randy joined Tay. "We ran into some trouble along the way."

Jezebel looked past the children. "Nothing too serious, I hope?"

Randy saw her attention had landed on his dad. He suddenly remembered that his father had not made the best first impression on the chess set.

"No... it *was* serious. But... but everything's better now. We're good."

Growing impatient, one of the rooks slid forward through the dirt. "Have you found us a new home?"

"We have," Taylor said. "There's a cabin not far from here that will be perfect."

"Splendid!" Adrienne exclaimed.

"It's important we retrieve our board from the ashes," a knight explained. "It's made of marble. I'm sure it survived."

"That's not the only thing." Randy turned to include the others in their conversation. "We should see if the mirror was destroyed."

The Librarian was puzzled by this. "The mirror?"

"The Looking Glass Alice uses to come into

Wonderland when she returns. If we hang it in this new cabin, maybe everything will be all right. Maybe she'll be able to come back like she's supposed to."

"Do you think that will fix the book?" Wesley asked.

"It very well could," the old man replied.

Excited to hear he'd had a decent idea, Randy started toward the torched remains of the cottage with Wesley. It took some time to dig through the soot-covered remains, but the boys eventually found the chess board and mirror just as they were hoping. When they did, each of the kids scooped up several of chess pieces so they could be carried to their new home. Some of the pieces were content to be carried. Others found it better to ride on shoulders. Douglas laughed when a few of the pieces climbed to the top of Randy's head.

While it would have taken the chess set several days on their own, with help they came upon their new home in under an hour.

"Oh yes," Adrienne said. "This will do nicely!"

The group filed into the small cabin to find it was set up very much like the original cottage. Randy and Douglas quickly began work to hang the mirror over the fireplace. Meanwhile, Taylor dragged a small table across the floor so it was centered in the seating area near the fire.

Jezebel watched from Tay's shoulder. "This will be just like home in no time!"

"That's the idea," Taylor reminded.

When the table was in place, The Librarian gently placed the chess board at its center. Stepping back, he watched as the pieces hurriedly began climbing the table legs so they could take their places on the board.

"How's that?" Wesley asked.

One of the knights rode to the edge of the table for a look at their new surroundings. "We couldn't have asked for better. We owe you a great debt."

Wes looked to Taylor beside him. "Sounds like we're even."

The knight offered an understanding nod then moved to join the group behind him. It made Taylor smile to see them so excited.

A bishop came to the edge of the table. "Would you be a lad and start a fire? I fear I've caught a chill after being outside the house for so long."

"Sure," Wesley grinned.

As Wes went to work, Taylor turned to find that The Librarian had moved into the cabin's tiny kitchen where he was rummaging through the cabinets.

"What are you looking for?" she asked.

"You friend Randy has me thinking. Now that we're here it may be wise to replicate the old cottage as closely as we can so everything's as it should be when Alice arrives."

A broad smile lit Taylor's face. "You're trying to find some cake."

"Correction..."

The Librarian pulled a pan from one of the cabinets.

"I've *found* some cake."

Excited, Tay pulled open one of the nearby drawers. "I'll see if I can find something to write on while you cut a piece."

When the two were finished, they had plated a rather large slice of the iced cake on the kitchen table with a small note beside it.

"Eat me," Taylor read aloud. "Perfect."

Wesley's fire was just beginning to crackle and pop when Randy and Douglas finished hanging the mirror. Both stepped back to admire their work.

Randy's dad smiled. "You did a good thing here."

"We promised them we would come back."

"Son, I think there are plenty of people in the world who would have used everything that's happened as an excuse to forget about these little guys. That's not what I'm talking about anyway."

Randy's brows came together in confusion.

"No one was thinking about Alice. No one had taken one minute to think about her story and how it might be fixed. Even the old man was in a hurry to get back to the library. But somehow… that mirror was hiding in the back of your mind this whole time… somehow you did the job we were supposed to do." Douglas shook his head. "Something tells me you're going to help fix a lot of my mistakes by the time you're through."

"Dad, what I said before…"

Douglas cut him off. "Don't apologize for telling the truth, Randy. Never. I've made so many mistakes, but somehow, through all of that, I did an okay job with you. But I never should have put you in a position where you were parenting me. You shouldn't be the one to tell me the difference between right and wrong."

"What do I know about it?" Randy gestured to Wesley and Tay who were saying their goodbyes. "There's a reason those two hate me, you know?"

"I know. But look…"

Randy's dad pulled *The Queen's Revenge* from The Librarian's satchel.

Only it was no longer *The Queen's Revenge*.

The gold foil stamped into the leather cover of the book now read *Through the Looking Glass*. When Douglas flipped the book open he found each page was a swirl of black ink and letters.

"The book is rewriting itself!" Randy exclaimed.

"It is now," Douglas said. "You did this. You, with your idea to move the mirror. So whatever there is between you and those kids. Whatever you've done to them, or they've done to you. It's nothing that can't be fixed. As for the difference between right and wrong: we'll work on getting better at that together."

CHAPTER 32

HOOK STORMED DOWN one of the castle's long corridors with Smee stumbling along behind him. A few of the Queen's men were lingering about inside the castle, but they paid the pirates little mind. The kingdom had fallen into chaos since the Jabberwock's attack. In fact, no one was even there to stop Hook when he pushed through the door into the Queen's chambers.

The flicker of three candles on a nearby table was the only light in the room. It was eerily quiet compared to the hustle-and-bustle of activity in the hall. The pirates had expected to find the Queen sitting on her throne, but she was nowhere to be seen.

"Where do you reckon she went, capt'n?"

"Something tells me she didn't go far," Hook explained.

"Yeah? How can you be sure?"

"She wouldn't know what to do if she'd run into the forest with everyone else."

Hook took the candlestick so he could see what he was doing as he explored the cold room. While nothing seemed out of place, he did notice something he hadn't given much attention before.

There was a large bookcase against the wall.

Hook had never been one for books and suspected the Queen likely felt the same way. But if that was true, why would she keep a bookcase in her chambers? Why stack dozens of books in rows like this if you never read?

He crossed the room for a closer look. Perplexed, he pulled several books from the shelf, allowing them to fall to the floor as he searched for any clue that might explain the bookcase's presence. Then he saw something on the floor—

Falling to one knee, Hook lowered the candlestick so it illuminated the tile. While most had been polished so they were perfectly smooth, a series of long gouges had been cut into the tiles near the base of the bookcase. About a foot long, they seemed to extend from the beneath the heavy piece of furniture – as if someone had pulled the bookcase away from the wall dozens of times through the years.

"What is it, capt'n?"

Hook rose to his feet "Take this, Smee."

He handed the candlestick to his first mate then rocked the bookcase back-and-forth, slowly scooting it away from the wall to reveal a tiny room where the Queen was hiding with her husband and the White Rabbit.

"Oh my!" the Rabbit exclaimed. "Please, don't hurt us."

Hook shook his head. "I'm not here to hurt you, friend. I'm here to help." He looked past the Rabbit and offered his hand to the Queen. "Your Highness…"

Still shaken, the Queen reluctantly allowed Hook to help her up. "I thought you might be working with the others," she explained.

"Of course not," Hook said. "And I hope I haven't overstepped my bounds, but I've ordered your men to round up those still in the courtyard. Most have fled into the woods, but I thought you might want to question anyone who remained to ensure there are no conspirators in your midst as there were with Alice."

"Well… of course," the Queen said.

"So you aren't working with Stanford?" the King asked.

"Not anymore. In fact, with your permission, I'd like to go after him now that I know the two of you are safe."

The Queen furrowed her brow. "You're free to leave when you please."

"I know that, but I was hoping we could come to an arrangement first."

"What kind of arrangement?"

"I'd like you to give me what Stanford was asking for," Hook said.

"You want control of my army?" the Queen asked.

"No. Of course not. They're *your* men. But I fear they need a competent leader if they're going to avenge the honor of your kingdom."

This was enough to make the Queen perk up a bit. "How do you mean?"

"Order me to lead an attack on the real world. I'll spill the blood of those who did this. I'll find the Alice child and bring her before you for judgment. I'll lead a march through their lands to ensure we are never the fodder to entertain children again. And when I'm finished, it will be just as we discussed."

"We'll rule," the Queen whispered to herself.

Hook's black eyes gleamed in the candlelight. "We'll rule as gods. And I promise: we'll never be controlled by words on a page again."

CHAPTER 33

AFTER BIDDING GOODBYE to the chess set, Wesley and the others started for the portal home. When they arrived, the kids couldn't help but think the old, dilapidated windmill looked ready to come alive in the moonlight – like a giant zombie hand with spindly fingers sprouting from the earth.

Douglas and The Librarian took positions near the windmill's entrance so they would be there to stop Hook and his men. Meanwhile, the children were asked to hide in a dense part of the forest nearby. They weren't happy about it, of course. Even worse for Wes, he'd had to relinquish his staff.

"I don't understand why we have to hide like this," Randy huffed.

"Your dad just wants to make sure we don't get hurt," Taylor explained. "What do they call it?"

"Out of harm's way," Wesley explained.

"Yeah. That..."

"We were two seconds from getting our heads chopped off."

"And he doesn't want something like that to happen again."

Wesley let the two bicker without any input from him. His attention was fixed on the meadow below. The forest was so dense he wouldn't be able to see much. For the adults below, spotting Hook and his men would be even tougher. In all likelihood, they wouldn't see the pirates until they were right on top of them.

"What if things go bad?" Randy asked. "Hook has six or seven guys."

Taylor grinned. "You saw your dad and The Librarian. I'm sure they'll be fine."

"Those guys were made of paper, Tay. Besides: Hook is different now."

Tay looked over to see if Wesley had anything to add, but her friend just moved his attention back to the cottage below. When he did, his face fell.

"What's wrong?" Taylor asked.

Wesley didn't answer. Confused, Randy and Tay shuffled over to see what had turned Wes six shades of white. Randy quickly pushed to his feet when he saw what was about to happen. He was ready to bolt down the hill to help but knew that wouldn't do much good. He'd never make it in time.

All he could do was watch and hope for the best.

❖ ❖ ❖

Douglas and The Librarian immediately fell into a defensive stance.

"You should see the look on your face," Hook smirked.

Smee stood at Hook's side, just a single pace behind his captain as always. The pirate's motley crew followed, but they weren't alone. Most of the kingdom's playing-card soldiers and armored guards had joined Hook on his trek through Wonderland: nearly sixty men to accompany Hook's crew.

"Isn't this how you envisioned it?" the pirate asked.

"Not exactly," Douglas said.

Hook motioned for everyone to hold back as he and Smee moved forward to address their adversaries.

The pirate looked about. "Where are the children?" he asked.

"Gone," Douglas blurted. "They've returned to our world."

"I'm surprised to learn you didn't flee with them."

"I'm only here to see you off, captain... back to Neverland."

"So you'll be providing me with the weapons you promised?"

"You lost that opportunity when you threw Hope off the balcony."

The pirate began to polish his infamous hook. "Yes. That. Smee will be the first to tell you that I sometimes let my emotions get the best of me."

"Oh," Smee chuckled. "That's true, capt'n. True indeed."

Douglas fumed, his emotions simmering beneath the surface.

The Librarian rested a hand on his friend's shoulder as Hook continued.

"It's true of everyone, I suppose. Even you. You've surrounded yourself with people you care for. One should never do that. You couldn't even bring yourself to hurt that young girl. Don't you see that's why you've lost?"

"You're talking like it's over. Maybe that's why you never win."

Hook gestured to the men standing behind him, a literal army of fairytale villains waiting to do the pirate's bidding. "It seems I'll win today."

"And what about Pan? You'll just leave him in Neverland, your great opponent? You'll give him the satisfaction of having Neverland to himself?"

Hook laughed. "You talk as if my battles with Pan were *real*. He's as much a prisoner in those bedtime stories as I've been. We suffered, so your kids could escape to a world of fantasy." Hook's words became sharper with each moment, knives unsheathed. "Well, that fantasy has become a reality, I'm afraid. We've leapt from the page in search of vengeance, and we'll have it soon enough. I'm going to burn every book I encounter in your world. Then I'm going to punish every child who's ever thought to get enjoyment from our plight."

"You're a madman if you think I'm letting any of that happen," Douglas said.

"And you're a fool if you think you can stop us. After all, isn't there a book within your library that will give me all the power I need?"

Douglas and The Librarian traded a nervous look.

"I'm going to rule your world just as the creator of Neverland ruled over mine. But don't fret. I'm going to allow you to witness my reign every step of the way."

"Why's that?" Douglas asked.

A dark grin split the pirate's face. "Because when I punish the children of your world, I'm going to start with your son."

Douglas felt his anger swell. The pirate had held a fire to his deepest emotions to ensure his rage boiled over. Douglas knew Hook was trying to goad him into a fight, but he wasn't going to sink to that level, he wasn't going to give Hook the satisfaction—

"No!" The Librarian yelled. *"Douglas! Don't!"*

Blinded by rage, it was only when his mentor called out that Douglas realized his pistol was already in his hand.

Smee stepped forward, knocking the weapon out of his hand before Douglas could squeeze off a shot. Hook pulled his sword, ready to bring it down on Douglas, its sharp edge descending in a deadly sweep until The Librarian blocked the blow with his staff. Weapons locked together, Hook's eyes narrowed when they met the old man's.

"Attack!"

❖ ❖ ❖

The children watched from hiding as Hook's army descended on the two men.

"We have to get down there!" Randy exclaimed.

"Give them a minute," Taylor said. "They'll be fine! Watch!"

Randy pulled away from Tay's grip but didn't move beyond that. Instead, he shifted his gaze into the valley, and his eyes widened so they were lit by moonlight and wonder.

Douglas and The Librarian were standing back-to-back just as they had in the Queen's courtyard. They threw magic with such ferocity it looked like they were painting the night. The stones atop their staffs left long arcs of vibrant color hanging in the darkness. Pirates fell to the wayside. Blasts of magic sent playing-card soldiers sailing in all directions as if part of a shuffle gone bad.

The heroes looked like wizards from another age, both using magic to battle evil against great odds. The whole thing brought a smile to Randy's face. All his life he had heard stories carried on whispers behind his back. People in Astoria talked about his father like he was the worst person in the world: a man who would do anything to get ahead and hurt anyone who dared get in his way. They talked about Randy's dad like he was the villain of their real world story. For a brief moment, Randy had believed them. But now, watching his father fight side-by-side with The Librarian, Randy knew better...

Douglas Stanford had been tempted to walk a darker path, an easier way that promised every-thing he believed he was after. But all of us are tempted from time-to-time. All that really matters is how we respond when darkness offers its hand.

In the end, this was his father's response.

"Wow!" Taylor explained.

"Yeah," Randy replied. "Wow!"

It was all he could think to say.

The boy's crooked grin lifted into a broad smile as he watched his father meet each of the approaching soldiers with a blast of energy from his staff. It was enough to light the entire valley until a single gunshot rang out. When it did, the night turned dark, and Randy's blood ran cold once more.

CHAPTER 34

THE ARMY'S ATTACK came to an abrupt halt, everyone frozen by the sound of the gunshot. The Librarian looked about until his eyes fell on Hook. The pirate was standing with Douglas's pistol in hand, a curl of smoke spiraling into the air from its barrel.

What followed seemed to happen in slow motion, as if a simple pull of that trigger had been enough to alter the laws of time and space. Douglas dropped to his knees. A thin ribbon of blood spilled from the corner of his mouth.

Randy screamed out from the hillside, drawing Hook's attention. The pirate looked up just in time to see Randy had broken away from Wesley and Tay and was now sprinting down the hill toward them.

"Well," Hook grinned, "that didn't go as planned."

Without thinking, The Librarian lunged forward, catching Douglas in both arms before his friend fell face first into the dirt.

The old man gently lowered Douglas until he was resting on his back.

"Don't move," he said. "Be still. I've got you."

Hook looked about at his men, a strange mix of pirates, playing-card soldiers, and armored knights.

"Do I have to do everything, you fools? Kill him!"

The Librarian clenched his jaw and rose to his feet. He turned to face Hook's army. They were ready to take him, but the old man wasn't having it. The stone atop his staff had turned a deep crimson to match his rage. He took a deep breath and slammed his staff into the dirt.

"Hyrugen!"

A sphere of red energy blasted out from the staff's crystal in all directions. It lit up the valley and left nothing but destruction in its wake. It sent the old man's attackers summersaulting out of control. It snapped trees in half and uprooted brush. Even the earth at his feet was disturbed, a crater forming with The Librarian at its center. It was like he'd dropped a bomb. And when the dust finally settled and the old man saw Hook and his men had been vanquished, he collapsed to his knees then fell into the dirt beside his friend.

◆ ◆ ◆

Short on breath, Randy dropped down beside Douglas. The boy's dread worsened upon seeing the blooming stain on the front of his father's shirt.

"Dad!" He pushed the shirt away only to pull his hands back when he saw the bloody wound in his father's chest. *"Oh my god! Dad?"*

"It's... it's okay... son." His words gurgled out of him like they were circling a drain. "This... happened... but... you have to go... get... get out of here."

Wesley and Tay finally caught up. Both slowed their approach when they saw the severity of Douglas's wound. Randy looked up at them. His expression begged for help. Taylor took a step closer, but that was all she knew to do. Meanwhile, Wesley knelt down beside The Librarian.

"Are you okay?" he asked.

The old man didn't look much better than Douglas. He hadn't been injured in the blast, but it was clear he'd used enough magic to drain him of all his energy. Wesley tried helping him to his feet, but The Librarian was so weak the boy wouldn't be able to do it on his own. *"Tay, give me a hand!"*

They helped The Librarian up as the murmur of injured pirates and playing-card soldiers wafted toward them from the distance.

"We have to go," Wesley said.

"I'm not going anywhere!" Randy growled.

"The Librarian can't fight and your dad..." Wes couldn't bring himself to finish.

"My dad's fine. You two go. Run if you want. I'm staying right here."

Wesley and Tay immediately recognized Randy's tone. It was the venomous voice of the boy they knew *before* their adventures in Wonderland, the voice of the boy that tormented weaker kids and made fun of good students.

Douglas spoke before any of them could respond. "Stop it, Randal."

"It's okay, dad. I'm here."

His father shook his head, his eyes glassing over.

"They didn't do this, son."

"What?" Randy asked.

Douglas laid a hand on Randy's arm.

"You... know... you already know who to blame..."

Randy recoiled a bit. "Dad, stop talking. Please!"

But his father wouldn't listen. "Randy..."

"Dad, you have to stop..."

"I... wasn't... going to do it... to help Hook..."

Douglas tried to say something more, but the words wouldn't come. Then his eyes dulled and there was nothing left behind the glass at all. His head slumped onto his shoulder. Douglas Stanford was gone.

"Dad? Dad!"

Tears pooled in Taylor's eyes. At her feet, Randy threw his arms around Douglas's lifeless body and began to cry in sobs muffled by his father's body.

Tay made sure The Librarian had his balance then moved to comfort her friend.

Wesley looked back to the tree line and saw their attackers were on their way to recovery. Already shaking the cobwebs loose, it wouldn't be long before Hook and his army realized that only three young children now stood between them and the real world. That would be enough to re-energize them in an instant.

"We have to go," Wesley said.

Randy looked up sharply. "What? No! We can't just leave him."

"They're coming back..."

"Good! Let them!"

"They'll kill us."

"They'll try." Randy grabbed Wesley's staff from the ground.

"What would your dad want you to do?" Taylor asked.

This was finally enough to give Randy pause. All at once the anger in his eyes was gone, replaced by a worry that suggested he thought his dad might already be watching. For the first time in a long time, Randy wanted to do the right thing – he just couldn't figure out what that was.

"Leaving now doesn't mean it's over," Wesley said quietly.

Randy looked down at his father's body. There was a peace in the expression on his dad's face that he'd missed before, a contentment.

"We can't let him get away with this," Randy said.

Wes looked him right in the eye. "I promise: we won't."

With that, Wesley hurried over to find The Librarian was holding out his amulet for him to take. Wes quickly snatched it and went to work, using the powerful talisman to open a portal in the windmill's doorway.

Purple light illuminated the valley as the doorway morphed into a pool of shimmering light. Taylor was already helping The Librarian back to his feet. Wes quickly moved to help, both children guiding the old man toward the portal just as its long tentacles of light started reaching into the forest.

"Randy," Taylor whispered. "It won't stay open long."

Still kneeling beside his father's body, Randy rose to his feet and looked into the distance. While his men were still struggling to recover, Hook had already pushed to his feet. The pirate watched Wesley and Tay hurry the old man through the portal. Then his attention fell on Randy, and the two locked eyes.

"So I take it you're the one," Hook hollered from across the meadow.

Randy backed his way through the portal, never once taking his gaze from the pirate. Even when his feet moved from the soft earth in Wonderland to the marble floor of Astoria's library, he refused to look away. Even as the portal closed between them, Randy made sure his face was the last thing Hook saw...

EPILOGUE

IT WAS STORMING in Astoria on the day the boy was finally adopted.

Most of the social workers had given up hope. He had so many strikes against him. He was a boy. Most couples look to adopt girls. He was older than average. Families usually look for young children, not teens. And he was sullen. While other children always did their best to make a good impression, it was like Douglas Stanford was trying to turn prospective families away. Or maybe after four years in the foster home he'd just given up hope like everyone else.

Douglas was sitting near the window when one of the center's social workers led Melina Rhodes into the rowdy playroom.

"That's him," the woman explained. "I told him you were coming, but..." Her voice trailed off, and she backed out of the room with a shrug and a frown.

Melina looked to the kids scattered all around her. Some were sprawled out on a fraying rug and playing with toys. Others sat around a table working on art projects. But most were clustered around an old television in the corner. She could tell the children were trying to avert their eyes, but they couldn't help but move their attention to the strange adult who had joined them. They all knew why she was there: she was there to save them. After all, anyone who looked a little closer would see their lives weren't as fun as they might appear. The toys were beat up. The art supplies were limited. The technology was badly outdated. The kids were laughing and playing, but it all seemed as muted and dull as the paint on the room's cinderblock walls – as if the kids were just going through the motions because that's what they were supposed to do.

Melina had taken it all in by the time she reached Douglas at the window. When she arrived, the boy's greeting was as cold as the day outside.

"You don't have to waste your time."

"I'm sorry?"

Douglas looked over at Melina. "I've been here four years. That's long enough to know you aren't looking for a sixteen-year-old. And even if you were, I ain't the one. So, like I said, don't waste your time. Don't waste mine."

The boy turned his attention back to the window before she could answer.

"I'm surprised you aren't playing video games with the others," Melina said.

"Never saw the point."

Unfazed, Melina gestured to a reading nook across from them. "Why aren't you reading then? Those books have to offer more entertainment than whatever's caught your interest outside."

"You'd be surprised," Douglas explained. "Besides: I've read all those books."

Melina arched an eyebrow. "Really?"

Douglas sighed. "Are we about done?"

A sad smile split Melina's face. "Why are you here, Douglas?"

"At this window?" the boy smirked.

"In a foster home."

This was finally enough to put a dent in the boy's armor. "What?"

"Why are you here?" she repeated.

Douglas pointed to the others. "Same as them. My parents abandoned me."

Melina grinned. "Really?"

Douglas hopped down from the radiator he was sitting on.

"You think that's something to smile about?"

"I think it's a lie you've told yourself."

Douglas waved the woman off and turned away. "Whatever!"

Melina walked over to the reading nook. She studied the books in the bookcase then ran her finger through the dust that had gathered on one of its shelves. Shaking her head, she fired a cold look at the boys fighting over a video game in the corner.

"It wasn't your parents who abandoned you," Melina said matter-of-factly. "It was The Librarian and his friends."

Douglas's mouth dropped open. His color faded. For a moment, his legs felt like they were going to give out from beneath him. "H-how do you know that?"

"I can help you get it back, Douglas. Everything they took, anything you want. We can make them pay for locking you away like this."

Douglas was completely unaware that tears were streaming down one side of his face. Either that or was just too caught up to care.

"I... I... don't understand... how do you know that?"

Melina took a book from the shelf then started back toward the window where Douglas stood. "We'll worry about that later," she said. "But if I help you, maybe you can help me. Does that sound like a decent arrangement?"

Douglas answered with a nod.

"That's very good," Melina explained. "I'll tell Ms. Sanders to get started on the paperwork right away. We'll get you out of here as soon as we can."

She tousled the boy's hair then started for the door.

Tears tracked down Douglas's cheeks. He felt like his heart was about to leap from his chest. He'd spent so many days looking out that window, all the while hoping he might see his family walk past. All he wanted was a look, now this strange woman was offering him a chance to walk into the house that had been closed to him since that heartbreaking incident four years ago.

She was offering what The Librarian and the Elders had refused to give him...

A chance to be himself again.

Melina was halfway gone when Douglas finally called out to her.

"Wait," Douglas said. "Who... who are you?"

"Well," Melina began, "Ms. Sanders knows me as Melina Rhodes. But I imagine you've heard me referred to by another name, one the Elders gave. So, feel free to call me Melina. Or if you prefer to be a bit more daring... you may call me The Muse."

TO BE CONCLUDED

ALSO BY ERIC HOBBS

ABOUT THE AUTHOR

Since his debut, Eric Hobbs has seen his work published by DC Comics, Dark Horse, and NBM. His debut graphic novel, *The Broadcast*, was nominated for the ALA's annual "Great Graphic Novels for Teens" list before being named "Graphic Novel of the Year" by influential website Ain't It Cool News. *The Librarian* is his first novel.

erichobbsonline.com
facebook.com/erichobbs

Made in the USA
San Bernardino, CA
21 January 2020